Jerrod Edson

THE MAKING OF HARRY COSSABOOM

Published 2000

Editor: Yvonne Wilson
Cover design: Dawn M. Drew
Cover Illustration: Chris Lloyd - Painting (Roofs of Saint John)
Typesetting & design: Anne Purdy
Author's photo by Nelson Rosa

Canadian Cataloguing in Publication
The Making Of Harry Cossaboom
  ISBN 1-894372-08-5

Canadian fiction (English) - Maritime Provinces fiction
Black humour - 20th century fiction

Edson, Jerrod, 1974

DreamCatcher Publishing
Suite 306 Dockside, 1 Market Square
Saint John, New Brunswick
Canada E2L 4Z6
e-mail: dcpub@fundy.net
www.dreamcatcher.nb.ca
Telephone: Toll Free 1-800-631-READ (1-800-631-7323)

Printed and bound in Canada

This book is for Leigh,

and for my mom and dad.

ACKNOWLEDGEMENTS

I wish to acknowledge Ernest Hemingway for teaching me everything I know about writing, and David Adams Richards for showing me that where you come from is what allows you to go anywhere.

I also owe thanks to my editor, Yvonne Wilson, for nurturing this book.

Jerrod Edson

ONE

***

Harry was drunk on the ledge in the rain. It was a cold January rain and the sky was grey and the day was dirty and wet. He could see his breath and he shivered as he stood unbalanced, his shirt darkened damp and cold on his skin. He held a bottle of rum and took a drink, the rain dripping from the bottle and running up his fingers over his wrist, then down into his sleeve. The rum was hot on his throat and he felt it warm in his belly after each mouthful. He wavered a bit before regaining his balance, then seeing his street below, Orange Street, he sighed heavily and watched the top of a car as it passed under him, exhaust smoking and splashing puddles as it went. He kept his stare with the car until it stopped and turned at the corner, then disappeared among the old brick buildings of the city.

Harry looked down between his feet, then closing his eyes, he bent his knees slightly and leaned out into the open air. I am ready yes, he said to himself. Ready ready ready. The rain hit his forehead and slid down his nose. He felt the water drip from his nose and onto the swell of his lips.

He was not ready.

Not yet.

One more minute.

Harry kept his eyes closed and took another drink. He thought of the city and the summer when the air was warm and the sun lit up his apartment. These were the good days. *I open the windows and the air flows through the apartment*, he thought and smiled. *And I can hear the traffic below and people clucking by on the sidewalk.* He smiled again for he remembered it so well he could see the brightness in his apartment and could feel the summer air and the fresh smell of the city in July. He remembered the day he met Catherine and how quickly she had come into his life, and how quickly she had left. And there Harry stood on the ledge in the January cold and rain, thinking of that summer day—

The city was hot in the summer and it was worse inside the bus. People sweating, sitting close together, quiet and drained from the heat, feeling what little breeze came in through the windows. Most times the bus would stop in the sun and there would be no breeze. Harry had a small portable fan he attached to the dashboard beside the steering wheel. And with the visor down over the windshield, his sunglasses darkening the glare, and the fan blowing up into his face, he was comfortable in the sun while he drove.

"I bet that fan makes the day go by quicker," a woman's voice said from behind him.

Harry kept his eyes on the road.

"It helps," he said. "Every little bit helps."

"Where did you get it?" the woman asked. "I've never seen a portable fan. I've got a small one in my apartment, but you need a plug."

"A buddy of mine gave it to me for my birthday," Harry said. "I don't know where he got it."

"Wal-Mart maybe," the woman said.

"Maybe."

"It gives a good breeze for being so small," she said. "I felt it when I got on."

"It works well," he added. "It's too damn hot to work without it."

"How long have you had it?"

"This is the first summer," he said. "My birthday's in February."

"You must have thought it odd getting a fan in the winter," the woman chuckled.

"I did at the time," Harry grinned. "But I'm thankful for

it now."

The bell rang and the woman got up and stood beside him, waiting for the bus to stop. She wore a pair of shorts that showed most of her legs, long and smooth, Harry thought as he made his way up from behind his sunglasses. Shopping bags dangled at her sides. Up her arms he went, until her face struck him suddenly. She smiled slightly, her upper lip curled, and you could see the bottoms of her front teeth between her lips. Her eyes were dark around the edges with long lashes and *striking*, Harry thought. He had never used that word before. Her hair was light, dyed blonde, and cropped short on her head, allowing her perfectly rounded jaw and delicate cheekbones to show her face in full.

Harry stopped the bus and opened the door.

"Goodbye," she said smiling, her teeth showing white.

Harry put out his hand.

"I'm Harry," he said.

She shook it.

"I know," she smiled again, looking down at the patch on Harry's City Transit shirt. "I'm Catherine."

She got off the bus and disappeared down the street. Harry watched her as he drove off. She walked confidently, the bags at her sides, in and out of the shade until he drove past her and down the street.

The next day, he saw Catherine again. She sat behind him. It was cloudy and the air was stale. Harry had the fan in his face as he drove.

"You know, I asked my buddy where he got the fan."

"Oh?"

"Wal-Mart."

"I'm smarter than I think."

"It was a good guess."

"A guess?"

"Not a guess?" Harry frowned.

"Sort of," Catherine answered. "Wal-Mart's got everything."

Jerrod Edson

"And now you know where to get one of these."

"I don't need it."

"You could use it at work," he said, his arms out long and twisting over the steering wheel as he turned.

"I could," she said. "On my desk maybe."

"Where do you work?"

"The high school," she answered. "I'm a secretary."

"Which one?"

"Saint John High."

"Graduated in '75," Harry said proudly.

"Me in '82," she smiled.

The bell went and Harry stopped the bus.

"See you tomorrow."

"Yes," she smiled, watching her feet as she descended. "Good-bye."

Harry had seen Catherine every other day for a month, talking for a few minutes before she got off at her stop. And every time, he had tried to ask her out to dinner, or out somewhere, but he couldn't find the right moment to do it. When she laughed, he felt as though he could handle all the heat summer could bring, as long as she was there behind him, her soft voice in his ear. But she would exit the bus before he could ask, and he would be disappointed when he drove off. Then she would get on the next day and he would be ready to ask her. But when she smiled his throat would tighten and she would get off before he could breathe comfortably again.

***

"You gotta go see her," Nick said, sitting on Harry's couch with a beer in his hand. Nick was Harry's best friend. He was a bus driver too. "You know where she lives?"

"She gets off in Millidgeville," Harry said. "But she might take another bus from there, I don't know."

"Then you go to the school," Nick said. "Go on a day

when you know she's working. Bring her flowers too. No way she'll say no. Women love flowers. When I get shit from Mary for not doing this or that, I bring her flowers and she melts."

"It's been a long time," he said. "I can't remember the last time."

"Then it's time…What, you afraid?"

"No," Harry quickly answered.

"Then go over to the school and ask her out," he said. "You want to borrow my car?"

"I can walk," he said. "If she says yes, then I'll need it."

"I didn't think the school stayed open in the summers."

"Me neither."

"Maybe she's lying."

"I don't think so."

"You know where to get flowers?"

"No," Harry said. "I don't even know what to get her."

"Roses."

"Roses?"

"Roses," Nick said. "From Peacock's over by the hospital. You get flowers for a woman, you get her roses."

"You sure?"

"I been married twenty years, Harry," he said. "I should know. You get a dozen roses, walk down there and give them to her, she'll say yes, guaranteed."

"I like daisies," Harry said.

"Daisies?"

"Yeah."

"Why daisies?" Nick frowned.

"They're simple. They don't say too much."

"Like you."

"Yeah, maybe," Harry said, thinking of it. "Like me."

"Roses are what you need."

"I'll decide when I get to Peacocks."

"Fine," Nick shrugged. "But if you're smart you'll get roses. Daisies are for country girls. Roses are for women."

"I think she's more of a daisy girl."

"She's a woman," he said. "And she's been in the city her whole life. You get her daisies and she'll think you're a moron."

"I don't think she will," Harry said. "I think she likes simple things. She'll like daisies."

"But you want this woman to say yes, you want to sweep her off her feet, you don't give her goddam daisies—you give her roses, like every woman wants. You go with daisies, you're taking a chance."

"Daisies are good."

"Fine by me," he sighed. "If I was a woman I'd want roses."

"You'd be a slut."

"But I'd still want roses," he said. "Not daisies."

"I'll tell you what," Harry began. "I'll pick up some roses for you when I'm there. How's that sound?"

"You are such a sweetheart," Nick grinned.

***

The corridors in Saint John High School were dark and empty in the afternoon. Harry stumbled along between lockers, holding his daisies, his footsteps echoing off the walls.

He knew exactly where the office was—or where it used to be. He hadn't been in the school since he graduated, and memories were catching up to him quickly. Just the smell of the place, that chalky smell mixed with cleanser brought him back to when he was young. He and Nick had once roamed these halls. They got caught smoking in one of the bathrooms downstairs, Nick ramming his cigarette down the sink when he saw the teacher walk in. He burned his finger doing it. Harry laughed out loud when he remembered seeing Nick's blistered finger as they walked home after school, his laughter echoing in the dark.

He remembered being cut from the hockey team both years. He thought he'd make it for sure in grade twelve. He could skate just as fast as the others, shoot and pass better than most. But they cut him. And Harry remembered seeing the popular guys on the team with all the pretty girls hanging from them. They wore ties on game days, and everyone knew who was on the team. Harry wished he wore a tie. Everyone would know he was a hockey player. He made his way through the darkened corridor and still wished he had played on the team.

When I get the transit service going, he thought to himself after picking out his old locker. *people will know who I am. I'll have commercials on TV just like Mel Quigley, and Big Johnnie Sebastian. It'll go, Christ, I know it will. People will know me all over the city.*

Harry held the flowers behind his back as he walked into the office. The furniture had all changed, the pictures on the walls were different; no blurry old picture of the queen between the two big windows. He remembered that picture well, the old hag with a smile, her crown shining gold on her head. The walls were still the same—cracked and old, the window frames with the dark wood that looked rotted, and the glass dirty from the outside and looking down onto Prince William Street. He remembered sitting in the chair outside the principal's office door —the same old wooden door— with Nick beside him bitching about his finger.

A thin, wrinkled woman with silver hair was sitting at the desk when Harry entered the office. He had expected to see Catherine right away and had taken a deep breath before he went in.

"Can I help you?" the silver-haired lady asked, her fingers resting motionless on a keyboard.

"Is Catherine around?" he asked nervously.

"She's in the lunch room," the lady said. "It's down the

hall, third door on the right."

"Thanks." He smiled, trying to hide the daisies as he turned and stepped back into the safety of the darkened corridor.

He had never been in the teacher's lunchroom before and after all those years he still felt as though he was entering a forbidden place. He took another deep breath and opened the door.

The room was surprisingly small. Catherine was eating a sandwich alone at the end of a long table. Empty chairs were scattered around the table. A small microwave sat on the counter beside the sink. A bulletin board stretched the wall behind Catherine, bare in the summer months save a few colored thumbtacks.

Catherine looked up and quickly brushed the crumbs from the side of her mouth. "Harry," she said oddly, and made him feel uncomfortable.

Harry stood tall and breathed out smoothly. He walked over to Catherine and sat across from her. He pulled the daisies from behind his back.

"I brought you these," he said and handed them to her.

"They are lovely," she smiled.

"I didn't think the school was open all summer."

"They do summer school here."

"Oh," he said. "Must be a fun group of kids."

"They're not that bad," she said. "Most of them just want to pass and get out and enjoy the rest of summer. I think when they come here, they realize they can't mess around like they did during the year, so they don't give the teachers any problems."

A moment of silence came and loomed between them. Harry felt the breathing heavy in his chest again.

"I was thinking maybe you'd like to go out to dinner with me," he blurted out. "Or if not dinner then maybe a drink."

"I would like that," Catherine smiled again, holding the

daisies close to her. "Dinner."

Harry pulled at his shirt, his best shirt he had. "I didn't want to ask you on the bus," he said. "That old uniform and all."

"You look handsome in your uniform."

"Thank you," he said, feeling a redness coming into his cheeks.

"You're welcome," she politely said, still smiling.

***

Harry borrowed Nick's car and picked her up the following night. She lived in Millidgeville, in the apartments by the university. They ate an early dinner at Grannan's. Harry was nervous and he chose his words carefully.

"It's a nice night," he said, looking out the window and down onto the Boardwalk. "No clouds."

"I like the summer," Catherine smiled. "I don't like winter."

"Me neither," he said. "I hate the cold."

"I went camping in the Bay of Fundy last month with some friends from work and we were freezing in our tents," Catherine chuckled. "We had to double up our sleeping bags to make it through the night. It was awful. It was so cold in the morning that nobody wanted to get up and make a fire for breakfast. But we did, finally; then it warmed up later in the day. The next night it wasn't as bad."

"At least it didn't rain," Harry said.

"No," she said. "We were lucky that way. There's nothing worse than being in a tent when it's raining. You roll over and touch the sides and get wet."

"I don't like the rain either."

"Do you ever go camping?"

"No."

"Not ever?"

"My father used to take me when I was boy."

The waiter came and Harry looked at his menu.

"Do you know what you're having?" she asked.

"I don't know," he said, then turning to the waiter: "Can you give us a few more minutes?"

The waiter smiled and went away. Catherine had her head in the menu.

"It all looks good," she said. "I don't know what I'm in the mood for."

"I feel like seafood. Maybe scallops or clams."

"Clams," she smiled . "That sounds good."

"Or maybe steak," Harry said. "Or lasagna. I don't know, either."

"Lasagna," she said. "It all sounds so good. I think I'll have the last thing you name. Name something else."

"Let me see here," he said, studying the menu. "Mediterranean steak—"

"Where is that?"

Harry leaned over across the table and pointed toward the bottom of the same page. "Right there," he said. "It sounds good."

Catherine read it.

"I'm getting it," she smiled.

"It's the only thing I've named."

"But it's the last thing too," she chuckled. "Everything sounds good."

"I think I'll get the seafood lasagna."

Catherine paused a moment, then sighed.

"I hate eating at nice places," she said. "It's too hard to decide."

"We can go to Wendy's," Harry smiled.

Catherine laughed.

"I think the seafood lasagna is what I want too," she said. "Just don't mention anything else or I'll change my mind."

Harry closed his menu. He was still smiling.

It was not quite dark after dinner and they drove out to Mispec on the winding road through the trees. They had their windows down as they drove, the crisp ocean air blowing through the car. The sky was red over the water whenever they could see it, for the road dipped in and out, in through the trees, then out along the ocean where they could look back and see the edge of the city in the evening, the lights of the port starting to show in the water, black against the sky.

They parked the car at the beach and walked down to the water. The tide was out and the sand was hard and rippled, the waves smoothening out over the sand as they strolled along. They climbed the big rocks at the edge of the cove. The rocks were covered in seaweed and they climbed carefully, the seaweed slimy green and slippery under their feet. They settled down close together, high above the beach and looking out onto the bay. A long ship sat still in the distance, far out in the open ocean and flat along the line of water and sky.

"Someday I'm going to have a house on the water," Harry said. "A nice house that looks out onto water just like this. Not like in the Valley either, not on the river, but on the ocean, where you can see for miles."

"It is beautiful," Catherine said.

"And I'm going to have a deck where you can sit and barbecue and watch the waves," he continued. "And maybe a boat I can take out fishing."

"You plan on winning the lottery?"

"I used to put my hopes on that," he said. "But not anymore. I got a plan that's going to make me famous in this city."

Catherine listened closely.

"There's no transit system from Kennebecasis Valley into Saint John," he said. "All those people working here in the city driving to work every day— have you seen the highway at suppertime? You can't move. All we need is four or five busses, drivers running twenty-minute routes, and you've got a business going. Then it grows from there, five busses to ten; then before you know it, I'll have a whole transit system covering Quispamsis, Gondola Point, and Rothesay. I just need to go to the bank and see about a loan. That's the hard part. Nick's got two kids who will both be in college this time next year and he won't risk anything. He said I'll have to get the money on my own."

"Do you think they will give it to you?"

"I hope so," he said. "I've had credit cards my whole life but never a loan bigger than a few thousand dollars. After they hear my plan I think they will. Nick's worried it won't go."

"It sounds like a good idea," Catherine said.

"It'll go," Harry said. "All them yuppies in the Valley. All you have to do is mention a money-saver and they'll pay. They'll load themselves in for work every day, load the kids in for the university, and leave the cars at home in the garage. We'll serve free cappuccinos. They'll love that. A fifty-cent drink for free and they won't get enough of it."

Harry stopped to take a breath. He had tired himself in excitement.

"I get going on about it and I can't stop," he sighed.

"It's good to be dedicated to something," she said. "Most people aren't dedicated to anything."

"What are you dedicated to?"

"My job," she answered. "It doesn't sound like much, but I am."

"There's nothing wrong with that."

"No," she said. "But it's not like you and your plans. I won't get rich from mine."

"I'm not in it for the money," he said. "Not entirely. Don't get me wrong, I want to make as much money as the next guy, but what I really want is to be remembered. And you know what keeps me going?…You just never know— I could start this service and it could grow and grow, then someday I'll be more famous than Elsie Wayne."

"She works hard. She changed this whole city."

"She sure did. She cleaned this place up real good. Remember what it was like before Elsie? Remember how dirty the waterfront was? And downtown, how dirty it was in and around Market Square?"

"It was pretty bad."

"I get people on the bus, tourists who haven't been here in twenty years," Harry said. "And they can't believe how beautiful the city is now."

"And now she's in Ottawa."

"Yes," he said. "Everything good in this province always seems to go west. But Elsie's always going to be a Saint Johner, no matter what Ontario does to her."

"She's a strong lady."

"She'll always be remembered," he said. "That's what I want. I want to be just like that."

"You will," she said. "I know you will."

"It's a lot to ask for."

"I would like my own house someday," Catherine said. "I don't like living in an apartment. I would like a yard that's mine, maybe a garden in the back where I could grow my own vegetables."

"What would you grow?"

"Oh I don't know," she shrugged. "I've never grown anything so it would have to be something simple. Carrots, maybe; I'm sure they wouldn't be too hard."

"I don't suppose," Harry said. "I would like my own yard too, just like this."

He looked out onto the water. The red from the sky was now gone and they could see the stars high up where the sky was black, far above the water. The flat line along the edge of the water now blended into the sky and all they could see was a slight outline of the ship and a flicker of light, but it was too far and too dark to see it clearly.

"I'll build you a house if I make it big," Harry grinned. "With a big backyard and a garden where you can grow all the carrots you want."

"I really hope you make it now," Catherine chuckled.

Harry leaned in quickly and kissed her as she smiled. Catherine was surprised, and she stiffened, then relaxed and put her arms around him.

"I would like my house on the water too," she said. "Maybe in the Valley."

"I wouldn't live in the Valley," he said. "Not with them."

"There are some beautiful homes down by the water. I would like to live there."

"Too many snobs," Harry said.

"I would ignore them."

"They would ignore you."

"Then it wouldn't be so bad," she smiled.

Harry leaned in and kissed her again.

"You make me happy," he said.

"Will you kiss me again?" she asked.

Harry did.

"Will you kiss me again?"

"You don't need to ask that question."

"Then kiss me again and again."

Harry did.

"And again," she smiled. Then with her mouth close to Harry's ear, she whispered, "Will you kiss me at home?"

***

Harry was embarrassed at the mess in his apartment. He had never thought Catherine would come home with him when he left to get Nick's car. His sink was full of dishes; empty soup cans sat on the counter beside the stove. Magazines, empty glasses and beer bottles covered the coffee table in the living room. His clothes were piled in a basket beside the couch.

"Laundry day tomorrow," he said.

He saw Catherine look around the apartment as she placed her shoes by the door.

"I'm sorry for the mess. I really didn't expect you to come over tonight."

"I can go if you want," she grinned.

"No," he said. "If you can live with it, so can I."

Catherine sat on the couch as Harry cleared the glasses from the coffee table and put them in the sink with the other dishes. He went to the fridge.

"I don't have much to drink other than beer."

"I like beer."

Harry smiled to himself as he pulled two bottles of Moosehead and went into the living room. He sat beside her on the couch.

"There's a baseball game on tonight," Catherine said.

"You watch baseball?" Harry asked and flicked on the television.

"I like hockey better."

"You drink beer and you like hockey," he smiled. "I think you might possibly be the perfect woman."

"I'm far from perfect," she smiled.

"Why didn't I see you on the bus before?"

"I just moved to Millidgeville. I used to live out by the airport. This is much closer."

"You should've had a car."

"I don't know how to drive."

"I'll teach you if you want," he said. "I'll borrow Nick's car and we'll find an empty parking lot."

"I don't think you know what you're getting into," she smiled, then: "Why don't you have a car?"

"Never needed one," he said. "Everything's right here. If I want to go to the mall, I'll hop on the bus."

"Do they make you pay?"

"We're supposed to," he said. "But nobody does."

Catherine saw a book by the end table behind Harry.

"What book?" she asked.

"*Nights Below Station Street*," he said. "Nick's wife

gave it to me."

"David Adams Richards," she added. "I saw him do a reading at UNBSJ last summer. He signed a book for me. Do you like it?"

"It's alright. I don't read much. But this guy, he's pretty good."

"He used to live on the West Side," Catherine said. "Before he moved to Toronto."

"Hope it doesn't change him."

"I don't think it will," she said. "He's true."

"Like Elsie?"

"Yes."

"I'll have to finish it then. Have you read any other of his books?" he asked. "I read the back and he's got quite a few."

"*Nights Below Station Street* is part of a trilogy," Catherine explained. "I've read all of that. I haven't read his hockey book, or his fishing book. But I've read everything else."

"He's got a hockey book?"

"You'd like it."

"I don't read much," Harry said again. "But I like this book so far. His language is easy. Not much happens though. He's not like Tom Clancy. I read one of his books, which one was it? Rainbow Six, that's what it was. Now that was a good book."

"I don't think Richards is anything like Tom Clancy," she said. "I think he's better."

Harry straightened himself on the couch. "Better than Tom Clancy? He's big all over the world. I never heard of this guy until Nick's wife gave me his book."

"He's not as big, but he's better," Catherine said. "He writes about New Brunswickers. Not many people outside the Maritimes care about that. That's why he's not very big. There's a difference between a writer and an author. Tom Clancy is an author. He writes bestsellers. David Adams Richards is a writer. He writes true works of literature."

"You're smart," Harry said.

"I went to university for two years after high school."

"I still never heard of him before that book."

"You should finish it."

"I hope he doesn't start writing about Toronto."

"He won't."

"Then why did he leave?"

"I don't know."

"People from Toronto are ignorant," Harry said. "I've heard them on the bus. Tourists laughing at how small everything is here. They should stay home."

"They're not bad people," Catherine said. "They think they're the center of the country because they are. They are bigger. They have all the money, all the sports teams, all the stars. We don't have any of that. I don't think we ever will."

"Because we're so small."

"I think so," she said. "You can't blame them for us being who we are, or what we are. We can't blame any-one but ourselves."

"It's impossible to keep up. They got all the money."

"Then that's the way it is," she shrugged. "No-one is to blame."

"But ourselves," he continued. "You said so yourself."

"If there's any blame to be given, it should be on us. Why blame someone else for moving forward?"

"Are we that far behind?"

"With certain things, yes."

"Like what?"

"It's nothing specific," she said. "It's our culture. You can't put your finger on something like that."

"I'm glad I'm a Maritimer."

"Me too," she smiled.

"I think it's good to be different."

"Me too."

"Whether we're behind or not," Harry went on.

"They are people just like us," Catherine said. "Toronto is their culture. Ontario is a different province. That doesn't make it any better."

"Like Tom Clancy."

"Yes."

"Then why do they think they are?"

"I don't think they do."

"Do you think they're ignorant?"

"About us, yes," she said. "But we're never in the news. We're the ones looking at them all the time. They are the centre of things, of everything. They look at themselves because everyone else is. How can you blame them?"

"I never thought of it that way," Harry said. Then after thinking a moment; "We have the AHL, they have the NHL. I like the NHL more. And of course they do too. Everyone does. It's bigger and better. It's too bad we don't have more people."

"I think we're fine the way we are."

"It would be nice to have an NHL team," he said. "Or anything they don't. Then for once they'd look at us."

"Maybe some of them do."

"I don't think any of them do," he frowned. "And that's why they're ignorant. I think they look down at us because we don't have the things they do, or the people they do. They're a lot like Americans."

"No," Catherine said quickly. "Americans are Americans."

"At least they have the excuse of being American."

"There's nothing wrong with having something all to ourselves," she said.

"I guess not," he said. "But it would be nice to be looked at every once in a while, instead of always being on the outside looking in."

"It would be nice," she smiled.

Harry picked up the remote and flicked to the baseball game. Jays vs. Dodgers. It was only the second inning, and they drank through the rest of the game. It was tied 2-2 right up to the end, when Carlos Delgado hit a home run in the bottom of the tenth that won it for the Jays. Harry and Catherine were both drunk, He leapt off the couch when he saw the hit, hugged Catherine tightly, and they kissed.

"Can you kiss me in bed?" she said softly, her lips pressed against his.

They went into the bedroom. Harry's sheets were on the floor, his mattress showing. Beer bottles surrounded the lamp on the nightstand. An ashtray full of butts sat on the floor beside the bed.

***

Harry lay in bed with Catherine close beside him. She was asleep and her head was resting on his chest. He could feel her breath on him as she slept, her arm soft and lying smooth across his stomach. He smiled in the dark. Catherine awoke shortly after, lifting her head from his chest.

"Will you kiss me again?" she asked.

"Stop asking that."

"Does it bother you?"

"No," he said. "It's just unnecessary."

"Then kiss me."

"Only if you don't ask."

"Kiss me," she grinned. "I'm not asking, I'm telling."

"And if I don't?"

"You don't like kissing me?"

"I love kissing you," Harry said.

"Do you love me already?"

"Is it too early to love you?"

"No."

"Then I do."

"Say you love me."

"I love you."

"Will you kiss me again?"

"Yes."

"I love you, Harry," she said. "And I love kissing you."

"Can you fall in love this fast?" he asked. "I never believed you could."

"Do you believe it now?"

"Yes."

"Do you love me?"

"Yes."

"Kiss me again," she said.

Harry kissed her softly.

"I never thought this could happen."

"But it did."

"Yes," Harry smiled. "It did."

"Does it bother you?"

"No," he said. "You?"

"I've never been in love before."

"But you are now."

"Yes, very much," she said. "And you love me."

"Yes."

"Do you believe it now?" she asked again.

"Yes," he said. "And I love you."

"Say it again."

"I love you."

***

The sun was coming into Harry's room when he awoke. He stretched his arms and yawned deeply, then turned his head to Catherine. She was lying on her side, her bare back showing. He leaned over and kissed the back of her neck. He lifted his head and saw the time on his alarm clock.

"Jesus," he moaned and got out of bed.

Catherine lifted her head from the pillow. "What's wrong?"

"I'm late for work," he said, looking around the bedroom floor for his pants. He found them and slipped them on. "I'm really late."

"It's only eight o'clock."

"I'm supposed to be there now," he said, buttoning up his shirt as fast as he could. He went into the bathroom and wet his hair under the sink. He brushed his teeth quick and back into the bedroom he went, sitting on the edge of the bed and tying his shoes.

"Will you get in trouble?"

"No," he shrugged. "But I've got to be at my stops at certain times. If I start late, then I'm all day catching up."

"Have you ever been late before?"

"Once or twice."

"And now you'll have to catch up."

"It won't take me all day," he said. "I'll make it up within the first few stops. It's just like anything else. When you're late, you drive faster; I don't sit the full five minutes at King Square, I get out quicker. Then I'll skip the first few stops. There's no other way. Otherwise I'd be late at every stop. It's better to skip a few at the start than be late all day."

Harry leaned over the bed and kissed Catherine lightly on the forehead.

"You go back to sleep," he said. "It's Saturday, school's out. I don't know what's in the fridge but help yourself."

He stood from the bed.

"Will you call me tonight?" Catherine asked innocently.

"As soon as I get home."

"Was last night because we were drunk?"

"Not for me it wasn't," he said.

Catherine laid her head back down on the pillow and smiled. Harry bent over and kissed her hard on the lips, then flew out of the bedroom. She heard the apartment door slam shut as she pulled the covers up over herself and went back to sleep.

***

A crowd had started to gather at the corner of St. Patrick and Union Street, right in front of the Aquatic Center. Many onlookers had never seen a real dead person before and they stared in awe with concealed excitement at the person who wasn't them.

The cyclist's dead stare made him look as though he was still alive, his eyes open and still, staring up into the sun. He was so fresh from life that his blood shined and seeped into the street cracks. His head was twisted oddly, his neck stretched, almost separated from his body. One side of his face had been peeled back, the flesh shredded.

Someone had taken the mangled bicycle off the street and laid it down on the curb. The front wheel was severely warped and the handlebars were twisted backwards. The pedal on the side where the bus had hit was smashed and crushed into the chain on the other side.

The bus was parked where it stopped. The front fender had a small piece of shirt wedged in the grill, but there was no other damage. Some passengers stood at the window, looking down onto the body that lay lit by the sun on the bright patch of the street.

Harry was standing next to the dead man with a blank look on his face, like someone had pulled out all thought and left him there. His mouth hung open, stupid and hollow, his eyes not looking, his legs holding his frame and nothing more. His wallet fell from his pocket and dangled from a chain attached to his pants but he never noticed. Everyone in the crowd did. It was the first thing they saw. The wallet hung alongside his pant leg and Harry paid no attention. The crowd remained distant, staring at him on the street. People drove by slowly with curious eyes and pointing fingers, but Harry saw none of them.

***

The bright summer sun had found a place in the city, and it was hot and sticky. The heat stayed under your clothes and you sweated heavily. Occasionally a slight breeze would swoop down between the buildings and you felt it cool across the swell of your back but it was gone as quick as it came.

A woman walked up Union Street in the heat. She carried two grocery bags and struggled along the sidewalk, in and out of the shade as she went. Occasionally she would stop and turn around, looking down Union Street at the intersection where the traffic had stopped. A police car flew by her up the middle lane, between cars and trucks and through red lights. Everyone watched and wondered where it was going.

Two kids scrambled past the woman, up the street in the direction of the accident, smiles and white teeth and full heads of hair bouncing with every step. The woman continued up Union Street, then stopped in front of a barbershop and placed the bags on the ground. She wiped her forehead on the sleeve of her T-shirt and sighed in the heat. Two old men stood at the door, long noses and big ears flapping in the sun, their heads turned down the street. The woman heard a radio playing from behind them. Soon another man, younger than the first two, popped his head out between them and looked down Union Street. He was taller than both and he hovered over them for only a few seconds before sinking back into the shade and out of the sun.

"Look bad, dear?" one old man asked, his long nose sniffing out in the sun.

"What happened?" the other asked.

"Someone was hit by a bus," the woman said.

"He alright?"

"I don't think so."

"He dead?"

"I think so."

"How'd it happen?" the old man repeated. "He really dead?"

The taller man came back out and hovered again between the two old men.

"What happened?" he frowned.

"Someone got killed down on the corner," the old man said.

"He was riding a bike," the woman added, rubbing the back of her neck.

"Damn kids," the other old man scoffed. "Damn kids and their bikes."

"Killed?" the man said with wide-open eyes. "You sure?"

"I saw him myself," the woman said.

"This, I gotta see," the man said excitedly. He squeezed himself between the two old men and headed down Union Street. The two old men remained at the door, their heads stretching down the street as far as they could.

***

People up on the other end of Union Street at Prince Edward Square had heard the sirens and seen the police cars. And downtown around King Square heads turned as sirens echoed off the buildings. The sirens could be heard all through the city.

The King Street Liquor Store was air-conditioned and the air hit you as soon as you walked in. The sun was on the other side of King Street and the store was cool and dark. Three slick pricks hovered in the back by the beer coolers, feeling fresh in the coolness.

some guy got splatted — fuckin bus.
shit.
yeah, laid him right out.

no shit.
was he dead?
oh yeah.
did you see him?
was he really dead?

By this time the police had moved the crowd back and were now directing traffic as cars took their time turning. A white sheet covered the dead cyclist. An ambulance was parked in front of the bus and two men were in the process of wrapping the body. The people in the crowd talked among themselves, pointing to the bus (now empty), then to the covered body, then to Harry who was sitting in the backseat of a police car, his legs on the ground, his elbows resting on his lap and his face in his hands. An officer knelt down beside him, writing down in a notepad everything Harry said.

Then Frank Beatrice arrived on the scene. People turned their heads when they saw him. Frank Beatrice didn't go into the crowd, didn't elbow his way through the muck. He stepped out of the van, adjusted his tie, looked into the camera and did his thing. The crowd turned from the dead cyclist. Nostrils popped up in the background while he spoke. Excited eyes wandered to the camera.

The heat got to Frank Beatrice too. He had a rag in his pocket and wiped his forehead and the back of his neck when the camera wasn't rolling. He had covered every news story in and around Saint John for almost twenty years. Many people had seen him around the city, but everyone had seen him on TV.

***

A young man who had heard the conversation at the liquor store held his wine tightly as he crossed Union and staggered down St. Patrick Street, then over the bridge that passed over the highway and looked down onto Harbour Station. He had seen the bus, now parked along the edge of the sidewalk by Market Square. And he had seen the body under the white blanket. A police officer directed traffic through the lights, around the area where the body lay.

The young man's roommate was plugged into the TV when he got back to his apartment. He was watching Frank Beatrice. A fan sat on the coffee table, air whirling around the room but making little difference in the heat.

"I just went by there," the young man said as he opened the fridge and stuck his head inside.

"You see Frank Beatrice?" his roommate asked, never taking his eyes from the TV.

"No," he answered. "But I saw the news van. Why don't you go over and see him for yourself?"

"Too hot."

"It is hot."

"Did that guy get killed?" he asked, now looking into the kitchen.

"He's dead. He was covered with a white blanket."

"I should go."

"It's probably all cleared by now."

"Shit."

He flicked the TV off and went into the kitchen where they filled two glasses with wine. Neither of them had to work until Monday and so a good drunk was in order. Drinking's a good thing when you've got good wine. They didn't have good wine but it got them drunk and that was good enough. They drank until late afternoon and then went back into the city for more.

They stood drunk, waiting to cross at St. Patrick and Union Street. They saw a few pieces of colored glass scattered and swept to the edge of the sidewalk. They also saw spots of dried blood, brown against the pavement. But the day had moved on and the afternoon was quiet and the corner was ordinary like any other. Cars stopped then went, lights green then yellow then red then green again.

It felt good being drunk in the afternoon. They joked and laughed on the way to the liquor store and bought their wine, three more bottles, and stumbled back across the bridge and up into their apartment, talking of the accident and wishing they had seen it.

***

That night the story was everywhere on TV. There was no interview with Harry but there was a photo, and Frank Beatrice told his background and the whole lot. He gave the whole scoop, leaving nothing out. He interviewed co-workers, City Transit officials, everyone. But Harry had been whisked away quickly by the police and Frank did not get to interview him. The victim's name was Devon McGrady, a third-year English major at UNBSJ. His family had been notified that afternoon.

Television sets were tuned in across the city, eyes glued to their sets in awe. Police were still investigating the accident but all fingers pointed to Harry. Soon after, witnesses came forward claiming the bus went through a red light when Devon McGrady was killed. Harry had tried to argue that he cut out in front of him and there was nothing he could do. But he had run the light, he knew. And he knew inside that he was wrong and that he had killed the boy. Harry was immediately fired and six long months would pass before his name was in the news again.

TWO

***

It was almost ten o'clock in the morning and the rain had made the day miserable. It was a dirty January day. In the city the streets were covered from snow that had come down heavy two days before. Cars moved slowly, their salty doors and smoking exhausts fighting off the cold and rain. People skimmed along the slushy side-walks, their faces hidden under hoods and tucked behind collars.

Harry woke up shortly before noon. He rolled over and reached under the bed for his cigarettes. He lay in bed and smoked, staring at the ceiling. From his bed he saw the gloom of the grey sky through his window. He saw the rain hitting the window and dripping down. His room was quiet and bare. The walls were pale and darkened from the little amount of light coming from outside. Harry smoked his cigarette and butted it in the ashtray on the floor. He rolled over in bed and went back to sleep until two o'clock.

The afternoon was quiet. The rain had stopped but Harry could see the sky still grey. He lay on his back and smoked another cigarette and looked about his room.

Jesus Christ, he thought as he smoked. *This room is a prison cell. If I had money I'd get a place with a big bedroom where the sun could come in and light the whole place. But this room, this fucking room never changes. The paint stays the same every day. These walls make me sick. Who would paint walls that color? That beige or white or whatever it is. Who the hell paints bedroom walls beige? How can you expect to wake up in a good mood with walls like these? How can you expect to wake up at all?*

His dresser stood erect beside the door, cluttered with change, wrinkled papers, a stick of deodorant and other assorted things placed without thought. Harry's eyes caught the bottle and the mouthful left at the bottom. He got up out of bed, twisted the cap and finished it off. His head was sore and dazed. He went to the kitchen, grabbed a fresh bottle of rum and poured a drink. The TV had been left on all night and so he flopped on the couch.

The day darkened more in the late afternoon and Harry remained on the couch. Catherine came with a few groceries and put them in the fridge. She sat beside him on the couch.

"What a day," she sighed. "What an awful day."

"What happened?" he asked as he flicked the channels.

"Just about everything," she said. "Three teachers called in sick and the supplies were late arriving. So this puts Bob Coterill in a bad mood right from the start. He ends up taking a class until a substitute shows up. He comes in cursing, slams his office door like a child. It's a long day when he's in a bad mood. I've been looking at my watch since nine o'clock this morning."

"It's a shitty day," Harry said.

"How has your day been?"

"I might paint my bedroom."

"That would be wonderful," Catherine said sitting up. "What color?"

"Don't know."

"When are you going to paint it?"

"Sometime."

"I could get some paint tomorrow after work."

"I'll do it sometime. Not tomorrow."

"I brought you some groceries."

"You bring any liquor?"

"No."

"Beer?"

"You know you should slow it down a bit."

"Jesus, not this again."

"Did you look for a job today?"

"No."

"I bought a paper," she said. "It's on the kitchen table."

"I'll look at it later."

"I bought some celery too. I remember you were saying last week how you wanted some."

"What would I want celery for?"

"You said you wanted some."

"When?"

"Last week."

"I didn't say that."

"Alright," Catherine said tiredly and sat back on the couch. "But I got you some anyway."

"You might as well take it home with you," Harry said. "It'll do nothing but rot here."

"You could try eating it," she sighed. "It wouldn't kill you to eat something good."

"It just might."

"Something other than liquid," she went on. "You look sick, Harry. You've lost weight in your face."

"I'm fine."

"I don't think you are."

"Christ Almighty, I'll eat the celery," he groaned. "Will that make you happy?"

"You don't have to be mean."

"I said I'll eat the celery."

Catherine started to cry. Harry went to the fridge and got a beer. He sat back down on the couch. Catherine wiped her eyes on her sleeve.

"I don't know why I bother, Harry."

"I don't know why you do either."

Nick stopped by around suppertime with a six-pack of Moosehead. He took one and put the rest in Harry's fridge.

"I got free tickets to the wrestling this Friday," he said from the kitchen. "You wanna come?"

"That sounds like fun," Catherine smiled.

"What wrestling?" Harry shrugged.

"WWF," Nick said. "Ringside seats. Mary won them at work."

"Where's it at?"

"Harbour Station," he answered. "You wanna come?"

"Maybe."

"We could shoot some pool first," Nick went on. "You know, have a few beers or whatever, then head on down."

"Sounds like fun," Catherine said.

"Then why don't you go?" Harry snapped.

Catherine's eyes began to water and she got up from the couch and went into the bathroom.

"This Friday?" Harry frowned at Nick who sat at the kitchen table.

"Yeah."

"I'll see."

"You gotta get out more," Nick said.

"I know."

"Then tell me you'll go."

"I'll see."

"You know Catherine is only trying to help."

"If she was trying to help she'd leave me alone."

"She's a good woman."

"I know."

"She comes here everyday to find you on the couch in your underwear," Nick continued. "And she still comes back the next day. Not too many women would stick around."

"It's her choice."

"You've got to help yourself," he said, flipping through the newspaper. "Look here: Snow removal, odd jobs, 8$ an hour, call 623-9792. It's probably *under the table*."

"I'm not getting up at six in the morning to shovel snow," Harry said.

Catherine came out from the bathroom. Her eyes

were red and Nick did not look at her when she passed by him and sat back down on the couch.

"How about this one," Nick continued. "Indoor painter required for light work, call 849-7771 after six. Doesn't sound too bad."

"A painter," Catherine turned to Harry and smiled the best she could. "You were talking about that earlier."

"I was talking about my own room."

"It's an *849* number," she said. "In the Valley. It could pay well."

"You got my car if you want it," Nick added.

"I'm not going to the Valley to paint some rich asshole's house," Harry frowned. "Spoiled kids running around all day and some snotty bitch watching every move I make. No thanks. And besides, they're cheap as hell— probably make more money shoveling snow."

Nick folded the newspaper and slid it away from him on the table. "There's more in there," he said. "You should have a look."

Harry lifted himself from the couch and stretched. His legs cracked when he stood. He went into his bedroom and came back out with his winter jacket. He slipped into his boots.

"I'm going to the liquor store," he said, zipping up his jacket. "Anybody want anything?"

Catherine and Nick did not answer. Harry closed the door behind him.

***

The next day Catherine called Harry from school. She was staying late to catch up on some work and said she would see him sometime after supper. Nick came by a short while later. He went to the fridge and took one of the Mooseheads from the day before.

"Grab me one of those, will you?" Harry said from the couch.

Harry had had a few drinks in the afternoon, and had just started on a new bottle of rum when Nick arrived. Nick gave him a beer and Harry smiled. He was feeling tingly from the alcohol and he relaxed on the couch and grinned. It was good feeling it come on slow and then into his head. It was good feeling it warm his arms. He looked at Nick who had been talking. Harry hadn't heard a word.

"So anyway," Nick said. "He needs a guy down there—just a few times a week."

"Where?" Harry frowned.

"The bowling alley," he said, realizing Harry hadn't been listening. "I was talking to Smitty and he said he needs someone a couple days a week. You got the job if you want it."

"The bowling alley, eh?"

Nick leaned over and looked Harry in the eyes. "It's a start," he said.

"A start to what?"

"A start," he said firmly. "I told him you'd be there before noon. He'll be waiting for you."

"The bowling alley," Harry said again. "What's that pay—six, seven bucks an hour?"

"It's better than nothing."

"I still got some money left."

"You're pissing it all away," Nick said. "It won't last forever."

"I'll get a job when I need one."

"You need one now."

"I don't need anything."

"How much money you got?"

"Enough."

"How much?"

"My rent's paid up to the end of February," Harry said. "I don't need a job till then."

"It'll take you forever finding one."

"I'll get one."

"Did you look at the newspaper?"

"Not yet."

"There are a few in there."

"I'll look at it tomorrow."

"All you gotta do is talk to Smitty."

"Smitty's an asshole," Harry frowned. "Remember that shit between you and Donnie McAlmon? Remember what Smitty did?"

"We were both drunk," Nick said.

"But he kicked you out and Donnie was the cause of the whole goddam thing," he said, holding his beer in the air as he spoke. "Donnie never should have taken a swing at you."

"He was drunk."

"And so were you."

"But that's just Donnie."

"Smitty should have tossed him out and left us alone," he continued. "And you know why Donnie didn't? You know why?"

"Why?" Nick said. He knew why.

"Smitty's afraid of him."

"I know."

"He's afraid of Donnie after he pulled a gun on Mike Baxter for fucking his wife."

"Did he really fuck her?"

"I don't know."

"Have you ever seen Donnie's wife?"

"No."

"She's not worth getting shot over."

"Mike Baxter," Nick said. "Now there's a guy who deserves to get shot."

"And Smitty too," Harry added. "Afraid of Donnie and so he kicks you out. Piss on Smitty. I haven't been back since."

"You should go see him," he said again. "You got the job if you want it."

"I'm happy here."

Nick got up from the couch. "I went down there myself," he said angrily. "The least you can do is talk to him."

"I'm happy here."

Nick sighed. "Don't ever ask me for a favor again."

"When have I ever asked you for anything?" Harry shot back. "I got some money left. I haven't asked you for a cent. When I do, then you can find me a job."

"So you can hide up here in this apartment?" he said. "Jesus Harry, you don't leave the place unless it's to the liquor store. You can't sit up here and feel sorry for yourself forever."

"Who says I feel sorry for myself? Who the hell says that?"

"I do."

"Leave me alone."

Nick went to the door. "You gotta get off your ass sometime," he said. "The sooner the better."

"Leave me the fuck alone."

"This isn't you, Harry," he said, his hand on the door handle. "You're not like this."

"Like what?"

"Like this," he said and looked around the apartment. "When's the last time you showered?"

"You want me to shower?" Harry snarled. "Is that it?"

"Go see Smitty."

Harry said nothing.

Nick opened the door and stood in the hallway, his head in Harry's apartment. "Go and see him," he said. "I know it's not much money but it'll give you something to do."

"I got plenty to do."

Nick slipped his head out and closed the door. He hadn't been there long enough to finish his beer. Harry got up from the couch and finished it for him. He sat back down and stared at the TV. *Damn that Nick*, he thought. *Damn that Nick all to Hell. I don't need sympathy from him or anyone else.*

***

It had been dark a long time before Catherine came. Harry was drunk on the couch. His bottle of rum half empty, empty beer cans scattered on the coffee table in front of him, he slouched, his head weaving in and about.

"I brought you some supper," Catherine smiled, pulling a plate from a Sobeys bag and putting it in the microwave. "Sorry I took so long."

"Where were you?"

"At school," she said. "I told you when I called…Are you drunk?"

"A little."

"I had some work to finish up on," she went on.

"Come here."

"Wait a minute," she said, looking at the microwave. "This is almost done."

"Come here and sit beside me."

"I got you something at the mall," she said.

"Give it to me."

Catherine handed Harry a bag. He pulled *Hockey Dreams* from it.

"A book?" he frowned. "I never finished his first one."

"You'll like this one."

"What did you get me a book for?"

Catherine grabbed it from Harry's hands and put it back in the bag. "I'll take it back then," she said. "I thought you would like it."

"When have you seen me read?" Harry frowned.

Catherine did not answer. The microwave beeped and she went to the kitchen and pulled the plate and put it on the coffee table in front of Harry.

"Maybe you will like this," she said.

Harry looked at the plate. Potatoes. Steak. Carrots.

"I made it for you."

"It looks good," he said solemnly. "How did you cook the steak."

"The way you like it."

"It looks alright," he said and began to eat.

"There's no celery in it," she said half-smiling.

Harry did not respond. He ate quickly, hardly chewing. Catherine sat beside him on the couch, flicking the channels as he ate. She noticed the bottle of rum and said nothing.

"Did you have a good day?" she asked.

Harry did not answer.

"Marjorie called in sick again," she sighed. "She's been out three days now."

"What's her problem?"

"She's sick, I don't know. I haven't been talking to her."

"Could be the flu," Harry said.

"Yes, maybe. It's going around."

Catherine was hesitant when she spoke again. "Did you do anything today?"

"Not much."

"Did you get a chance to look at the paper?"

"No."

Catherine flicked the channel.

"Nick was here," he said.

"Oh?"

"He got me a job at the bowling alley."

Catherine perked up on the couch. "That's wonderful!" she smiled. "When do you start? I'll come down and see you."

"I have to talk to Smitty."

"Then go talk to him."

"Smitty's an asshole."

Catherine lost her smile. Harry poured some more rum into his glass and sipped.

"What's it doing?"

"Don't know," he said. "Cleaning shoes, taking money,

I guess."

"It was good of Nick to do that."

"You don't know Smitty."

"Who cares about him," she said, sitting up again. She was reluctant to smile. "Go down there and take the job. It'll feel good to get out."

"Smitty's the kind of guy who would stab you in the back in a second," he said. "I don't want to work for him."

"Couldn't you go down there?" she pleaded. "Couldn't you go down there and take the job? See how it feels. If you don't like it, you quit, simple as that. But at least give it a try."

"It pays minimum wage."

"That doesn't matter. It's still something."

"It's not much."

"It's better than nothing," she said. "It will get you out of this slump."

"Slump?" Harry frowned.

"It will get you out of this apartment."

"You sound like Nick."

"He's just trying to help."

"I don't need anybody's help," he said. "How many times do I have to say that?"

"You don't have to say that," she said calmly, then resting her hands gently on her knees, she sat back.

"Yes I do," he said, raising his voice. "I'm saying it all the time. I've got my own problems. Let me deal with them. You and Nick don't know shit, okay? It might make you feel good if you come here with a bag of groceries and always smiling, but it doesn't make me feel any better. You think it's easy for me to see you so goddam cheerful all the time?"

"I didn't know you felt that way," she said.

"Well now you do," he snapped, his mouth full of food and the words deep and unclear. "I don't need your help, or Nick's help, or anybody else's. I can't even sit in my own home without people bugging me. Is that too much to ask?"

Catherine was cautious about answering.

"Is it?" he asked again, looking at her straight, his eyes drifting off slightly in his drunkenness.

"I didn't know I bugged you," she said. "I won't come over anymore if that's what you want."

Harry chewed his food, then sipped on his rum. Catherine sat uncomfortably still, looking at the carpet. She got up slowly from the couch, went to the kitchen and grabbed her jacket, then quietly slipped out of the apartment. He heard her tying her boots as he scraped the last of the potatoes onto his fork. He heard the click of the door as it closed, the lock clicking gently. He sank into the couch, resting the glass of rum on his belly. The room was spinning a little now. He sat, staring into his glass, his chin doubled on his chest.

What time is it? he thought; then, *What does it matter? You old fool. It doesn't. When tomorrow comes, it comes, and you deal with it then. No sense worrying about it now. No sense waiting like a scared kid under the sheets. No, tomorrow is tomorrow and I'll leave it till then.*

He thought of waking in the morning, of hiding under his sheets, wishing the day would go quickly and stay away from the safety of his bed and his sleep. He thought how he felt as he woke each morning, of wishing he wasn't there, that he would be anywhere but in his bedroom with his walls, pale in the morning light. *No no no,* Harry thought on the couch, *tomorrow's not here yet. Not* yet. He twisted his head around and squinted at the clock on the wall beside the fridge. *9:35. No, tomorrow is far off old man. Far off.* Then he thought of Smitty and the bowling alley. *Damn that Nick.* He rested his head on the back of the couch, closed his eyes and breathed deeply through his open mouth, the glass of rum locked between his hands.

***

Harry lay stiff on the couch when morning came. He could see the day dirty through the window. His side was moist with rum, the glass lying on the couch beside him. He first thought of Catherine, remembering the night in Mispec. He remembered the ship far out, and the way Catherine had first stepped back when he kissed her, then leaned in against him when he kissed her again.

Then he thought of Nick and the false lining that grew between them, between the words, the looks and smiles. It had planted itself between what they once had as friendship. Harry lay on the couch, stretching out, his back aching. *Nick never should have talked to Smitty,* he thought. *Why Smitty?* He lifted himself up and went to the bathroom and pissed. He showered and brushed his teeth. And Harry damned Nick once more before dressing and making his way down to the bowling alley.

A mist fell as he walked down Orange Street. Dripping garbage bags lined the curb. The sidewalks were patched with slush and puddles. He cut through King Square, passing under the tall trees and by the fountain, the snow covering and running smooth across the fountain as he passed. There were many footprints going all directions in the snow along the path that led to the movie theatre. Harry skimmed across the street, then down Charlotte and finally onto Union Street, where he crossed between cars stopped at the lights.

He shivered, his hands tucked in his pockets, his arms tight against his body. His chin was hidden under his collar and he watched each foot as it stepped and splat the ice and snow along the sidewalk. He walked a few minutes before he looked up and saw the bowling alley in front of him. He stopped suddenly when he saw, down the street, the corner of St. Patrick and Union.

For a moment, the winter disappeared and the summer came hurtling into his memory. He was driving the bus, a smile on his face as he thought of Catherine and where they would go after his shift. He was almost caught up to his route. *It happened too fast,* he thought. *I couldn't do anything. Nobody could. He should have waited; he should have waited at the lights with the cars. It happened all too fast.* He remembered feeling the bus jolt when he turned the corner, watching the light go red before he made the turn. He locked the brakes when he saw Devon McGrady fly out from under the bus, hitting the road and skidding onto the middle of the intersection. His body did not move when it stopped. *Too fast,* he thought, shaking his head in the cold, trying to rid himself of the picture of Devon McGrady lying on the road in the morning sun.

Harry turned and looked up Union Street and saw people scrambling about, shivering in the cold as he had moments ago. He had walked right by the city busses parked at King Square, but he was staring at his feet and hadn't seen them. *I wonder if they saw me,* he thought. *Didn't any of the drivers notice me crossing the street? Did anyone notice me at all?*

Harry saw himself in the glass doors of the bowling alley. *I look old,* he thought. *I am old. And here I am, and Smitty inside, him smirking because he knows I need him. He's like that; he'll always smirk when he tells me what to do. He'll smirk when he gives me my paycheck because he knows how much it is, how little it is. And he'll smirk whenever he sees me, that prick. There's no luck in the world for me. I attract shit.* He stood for a moment silent. *Smitty won't smirk at me ever.* He turned away from the doors and walked back home where he sat alone in his apartment.

***

Catherine did not stop by. Harry wanted to see her. He felt a hollow ache in his chest when he thought of her. He watched TV all afternoon, finishing his bottle of rum before walking down to the Prince Edward Square liquor store for another. He returned and drank heavily, and thought of Catherine again. He wished he had gone inside and talked to Smitty. *I wish I could have the day back*, he thought, his drunken mind wrapped up in the morning. *All I had to do was go inside and see him. I could have called Catherine and told her by now. She would be here now. And I could call Nick and things between us would be good again. There is just no luck. Jesus, I wish I had the day back. But the day is gone, you fool, and look at you now. It's the middle of the night.*

Harry got up and looked out his window. The street below was dark and quiet. It was snowing lightly and the pavement shined from the streetlight on the corner. The sidewalks were smoothed over white. Harry stood with his nose pressed against the cold window, his breath fogging his view of the cold night. He retraced his walk to the bowling alley in his mind. This time he saw people, saw the cars and the parked busses. He stumbled to his bedroom and fell asleep with his clothes on, his last thoughts of Catherine and wishing she had stopped by.

The phone had rung a few times before Harry woke. He rolled over in the dark and fingered his way around the night table until he found it.

"Hello?"

Hello, Catherine's voice muttered over the phone.

"What time is it?" Harry asked, his throat dry and coarse.

Almost two-thirty, she said. *I'm sorry for waking you.*

"You didn't come over today," he said.

No.

"Are you coming over now?"

No.

"Why are you calling?"

There was a moment of silence before Catherine spoke. Harry heard her crying on the other end. She composed herself and breathed calmly.

I don't know anymore, Harry, she said

"About what?"

Us. she replied.

Harry listened carefully.

I have been crying in bed all night. I can't take this anymore. I try and I try but I'm getting nowhere. You are not an easy man to be with. You must see that, don't you? I know things have been hard for you but surely you must see how people are trying around you. Don't you see that?

Harry said nothing.

Every day I try to see you, try to put a smile on your face but nothing works. Do you know when I'm happy? When I'm at work. People talk to me; they smile at me, and I can forget about feeling sad because I know you're in that apartment drunk. Everyday I walk to your place trying to think of something that might bring a smile to your face. And for that short time it takes me to get to your place, I have some hope that maybe this time I will see the Harry I met. But I never do. I see the same thing every day; and every day I leave early because I just can't take it. It has been going on too long.

"I'll change," Harry said.

No. Catherine sobbed. *No you won't. I have waited too long for you to change. I have cried myself to sleep too many times and it has to stop.*

"I'll try, I will," he said.

I have given you more chances than you deserve. I'm thinking of me now, Harry. This is what I need.

"I'll read that book," he said. "I'll read the whole thing tomorrow."

It's not about that. It's been going on a long time now. I fell in love with you in one night, she said. *But it has taken me six months to fall out of love.*

"I will change," he said again. "I went down to the bowling alley today."

Catherine paused a moment.

Did you get the job?
"No."
What did he say?
"I didn't talk to him."
He wasn't there?
"I didn't go in."
You will not change, Catherine repeated, the hope in her voice gone again.
"You don't understand," Harry said. "I was there and--"
I'm not listening, Harry. Not anymore. Please understand why I'm doing this. I tried, I really did, but I can't do it anymore.
"You don't care," he said. "You leave me like this."
It's not that. You know it's not that.
Harry sighed. He knew.
Good-bye, Harry.
He hung up the phone. He felt a weight in his chest, pressing on his lungs as he breathed. He lay in bed in the dark, his eyes open and looking at the shadows on the ceiling from outside.

***

It had been raining since dawn. It was cold again and the early morning street was alive and people hurried along the sidewalk. The rain tapped at Harry's window. He rolled over and lit a cigarette. He would go down to the bowling alley and see Smitty. See if he could straighten things out. *I'll think of something*, he thought in bed, the rain hitting the window and dripping down.
The rain was falling steadily as Harry walked along Orange Street. The snow was dirty and had gone down since yesterday. He made a point to notice things, to notice the parked busses and see if Nick was there. *I'm not losing myself in my thoughts*, he thought. *Not today. That stuff gets you into trouble. Stay away from that stuff, old boy, and things will go right. I'll talk to Smitty. I'll get*

the job and call Catherine at school. Maybe I could walk over and surprise her. Yes, he decided, feeling good when he thought of it. *I will do that.*

He passed through King Square with his head up. He looked up at the old trees, black and naked in the snow. Some pigeons hid from the rain under the benches, their tiny prints in the snow around them. They were dirty and wet but still beautiful in the ugliness of the rain and snow and salt that covered everything salty white and dripped down and made puddles in the street. Harry crossed the street by the bus stop. Three busses were sitting but none was Nick's. He recognized one of the drivers and turned his head quickly not to be noticed.

By the time he got to the bowling alley, the rain had flattened his hair. He shook the rain from the arms of his coat and opened the glass door without looking. He flipped his bangs to one side and neatened his hair the best he could.

The bowling alley was quiet and empty. It was warm but Harry's hands were cold and he rubbed them on his pants. Three old men sat in the middle lane lacing up their bowling shoes. They were talking about the rain as he walked by. He went to the counter where an acned teenager stood.

He looked at Harry. "Can I help you?" he asked and Harry could hear a nervousness in his voice

"Where's Smitty?"

"He went out for a bit," the teenager said. "We ran out of Coke."

"You sell that here?" Harry joked but the teenager didn't flinch.

"I can give you your shoes if that's what you want," he added. "I just don't know how to ring it in yet. I'll give you the shoes and I'll write it down. That's what I did with them." And he pointed to the old men who were now standing and about to bowl.

Harry looked around the bowling alley. It was bare and

he'd never been in there that early in the day and had never seen the place so empty. He turned back to the teenager who stood erect and waited for Harry to speak.

"You don't know how to ring it in."

"No sir," he answered. "This is my first day."

"I see."

"He said he'd be back in a few minutes."

Harry turned from the counter and walked out into the rain. He cut down Germain Street, then up King Street, stopping to buy a bottle of rum. He hiked through King Square and finally onto Orange Street. He hadn't noticed the busses or the pigeons or the trees. He walked quickly, his bottle tight in his hand. He got back to his apartment, threw his wet coat on the floor, sat on the couch and was drunk by noon.

It's too early to be awake, he thought. *This awful day and this goddam apartment. And this miserable winter, the shit and muck you have to step in to get somewhere.*

He thought of Smitty and of the new kid and he knew that could have been him behind the counter, with a job. He knew Nick was right when he told him it was a start. And he knew that he had missed his start and could not get the day back.

Stupid punk kid, Harry thought, almost saying it aloud. *Should be in school. He didn't look twelve. Zit little bastard. No no, you shouldn't blame him. It was Smitty. He knew I would be coming. He knew I would see the kid. Miserable prick, probably at the bowling alley smirking right now.*

He poured the rum into the glass, filling it full. He took a big drink at the start and looked at the glass to see how much he had drunk. Then he sat with the glass cupped in his hands and stared at the bare walls as the rum tingled in his belly.

By mid-afternoon Harry could hardly stand. He leaned across the couch and looked down onto the street. He could smell the rum on his breath as he breathed against the window. The rain had stopped but a drizzle made the day dirty again. A thin delicate woman skipped across the street, tucked under an umbrella. Harry watched her jump the puddles and skip onto the sidewalk and slip away around the corner.

She looks like Catherine, he thought. He waited for someone else; someone else who looked like Catherine. But no one else came. *Catherine isn't coming*, he thought. *She's not coming. Maybe tomorrow.* He paused a moment. *No, you try to fool yourself but you're smart. You're hard to fool on days like this. Catherine isn't coming today. Or tomorrow. You're a hard fool.* The street was empty in the afternoon and he plopped back down on the couch and felt the sadness that came when he knew another day had passed without him.

He took one last mouthful of rum and finished the glass. It was hot on his throat and it made his eyes water. *There will be no more days like this*, he thought. *No more. What's a man to do? Is tomorrow going to rain? Probably. And the next day and the next. You are a hard one for luck. Yes, a hard fool and a hard one for luck.*

Harry stood and was stunned by the sudden drunkenness that came into his head, and then settled in his legs. His head was spinning but soon cleared and he felt the warmth of the alcohol again. It was in his arms now and down his legs and into his feet.

He walked out of his apartment and down to the first floor. The mailboxes were by the front door, against the wall. Harry could see the drizzle through the door. He sighed when he saw it. He opened his mailbox and pulled out his mail, the bottle of rum tucked under his arm.

NBTel.

Visa.

Royal Bank.

He did not want to open any of them.

Suddenly the front door opened and in walked Charlie

Foster, a milkman who lived down the hall from Harry. He was always drunk in the afternoon after his shift and this afternoon was no different.

"Hello Harry," he said.

Harry could smell the liquor on Charlie. Or was it on himself? It didn't matter.

"Hello Charlie."

"Shitty day," Charlie said, opening his mailbox. He fumbled with his keys, then missing the slot until he finally got it, reached in and grabbed his mail. "I've been soaked since five o'clock this morning. Goddam weather."

"It is shitty," Harry said.

Charlie went up the stairs, sorting through his mail. He tripped on the first step, the mail scattering at his feet. He swore jesus fuck and picked it up, then swore again christ mary shit and continued up to his floor.

Harry looked outside.

Tomorrow will not rain, he thought. Charlie lost his footing once more and he swore christ fuck jesus mighty. Harry heard his door close. He looked outside again and saw the drizzle. *I won't let it rain. Tomorrow there will be sun, and the snow and shit will be gone. It'll all be gone. I'll let it all go away. Yes, dear me, there's something good of this day after all. There won't be another tomorrow like this.*

His body was heavy as he stumbled up the stairs. *No more muck and shit*, he thought as he pulled himself up the staircase, the envelopes held loosely. *No more fucking bills and no more money. Gifts make people feel good. Or do they? Yes yes, they certainly do. And this will feel good, this gift I'm giving myself. It'll all feel good and the day will be no more.* Harry did not stop on his floor. He went up to the next floor, then up one more, then past the top floor, each step a little heavier than the last.

***

Of all the years Harry had lived in his small apartment, he had never been on the roof. He kicked open the door and stepped outside, stumbling a bit on the door edge, then gathering himself abruptly. He stood still for a moment, looking across the city rooftops. He did not have his jacket and soon the drizzle turned to rain and he felt the wetness heavy in his shirt. But he did not feel cold. The apartment was stuffy in the winter with dry stale heat, and now being outside, the water was cool and fresh on his face.

The fog did not allow Harry to see very far, but he squinted in the direction of the water, trying to get a glimpse of the toll bridge that stretched across the Saint John River that separated the West Side of the city from the East. *I wish the bridge lights were on*, he thought. *I could see it if they were. But you're too goddam early for the lights. They won't come until after supper. They won't come until late when it's dark and the day is almost over.* He twisted his wrist around and focused carefully. *3:20. The day is far from over.*

Harry looked to his left toward the open water in the hopes of seeing the dry dock that had once flourished with shipbuilding but was now desolate and still. He thought of Mispec and the winding road through the trees. He turned back, looking toward the toll bridge, then beyond it to the Reversing Falls bridge, and not far from there, the pulp mill with clouds of smoke blowing up into the sky; the long trucks coming and going. But he could not see these either and he imagined what they would look like on a clear day.

A lot of people have jumped from Reversing Falls Bridge, Harry thought. *And their bodies don't get found for months. What's the use of that? If you must jump, then jump. Why bother with all the trouble driving out there and drowning in green Irving water? It's the water that kills, I suppose, not the fall. But if it's done right, it should be the fall that does it. Drown yourself in the tub if drowning is the way. Reversing Falls is unoriginal, and too damned much trouble.*

Harry took a drink of rum and looked down Orange Street. Above the old brick buildings he saw the tops of the old trees in King Square. He thought of the pigeons around the fountain and under the benches. And not far from there he could see the area where the bowling alley was. He looked up into the clouds and took another drink.

He was slow and careful when he lifted himself up onto the cement ledge and stood. He leaned off balance and his arms swung out and he caught himself and straightened out. *Now now dear fellow, you dear dumb shit*, he thought. *In a hurry and it won't be done right.* He looked down at his feet and saw the street below, the flat tops of cars and the metal tops of the streetlights. He held the rum tightly in his hand.

He sighed heavily and watched the top of a car as it passed under him, exhaust smoking, splashing puddles as it went. He kept his stare with the car until it stopped and turned at the corner. Harry closed his eyes, then bent his knees slightly and leaned out into the open air. *I am ready yes*, he said to himself. *Ready ready ready.* He felt the rain hit his forehead and slide down his nose. He felt the water drip from his nose and onto the swell of his lips.

He was not ready.

Not yet.

One more minute.

He thought of Devon McGrady.

He thought of him there on the pavement. He saw the red light; saw it and went like he always did. Devon McGrady had been with Harry since that day. And Harry had tried his best to rid himself of the memory but there was nothing he could do. He was always there, behind every glass, under every breath, between every blink.

Now Harry saw everything in that day; could smell the

summer air and the sweat of the city, the crowd that gathered at the corner as he drove off in the police car, their wide-eyed glares and excitement when they saw the body on the street, the children staring down in awe, the cars driving slowly by.

Harry saw the bike mangled and the wheel warped and blood in the spokes. He saw Devon McGrady's legs, flopped and scratched, and his eyes staring up at the sky, his blood soaking into the pavement and shining in the sun. He saw his bus and the grill with the blood drying on the metal, the piece of shirt in the grill, and the sunlight in the metal against the blood.

Christ Jesus, he thought on the ledge. *Christ fuck almighty.*

He kept his eyes closed and took another drink. He thought of the summer when the air was warm and the sun lit up his apartment. These were the good days. *I open the windows and the air flows through the apartment.* He smiled. *And I can hear the traffic below and people going by on the sidewalk.* He smiled again, for he remembered it so well that he could smell his apartment and the summer air and the fresh smell of the city in July. He remembered the day he met Catherine and how quickly she had come into his life, and how quickly she had left. He wished he had gone out onto the roof then and seen the river and the bridge, and the West Side of the city.

Summer is a long way off, old boy. Too far off. This winter has not yet even begun. February and March are cold and dirty and they aren't even here yet. The summer is a long, long way off.

Harry opened his eyes and looked to the right. *But I have to settle for you, dear trees*, he said out loud, holding his bottle toward King Square. *You don't need to be ashamed dear trees. I'm perfectly fine with seeing you right now. A tree is a symbol of life, isn't it? Is it?* He paused. *You old fool, talking to trees. You old foolish* bastard. *When have you ever known a symbol of any-thing?* He closed his eyes again and tried to remember summer.

Harry opened his eyes when he heard a noise from the roof across the street. He did not smile. He felt the cold and was shaken on the ledge. He saw two men, one with a camera setting up a tripod, and the other holding an umbrella, his face hidden. Then, suddenly, the man with the tripod saw Harry, and soon the man under the umbrella turned and looked at Harry, who held his rum.

Harry did not move. He looked at the men and for a moment nothing happened. He stood on the ledge and stared across the street, the water now heavy in his clothes and dripping into his eyes.

***

When Frank Beatrice saw Harry standing on the ledge, his heart started to race. He looked at his camera-man.

"Get that camera ready," he said sternly, and stood in awe and held his stare with Harry. "Hurry up."

"Who is it?"

"Please," Frank Beatrice said. "Just do it."

"Who is it?"

"I don't know."

Frank Beatrice squinted into the rain. He had seen that face before— that rounded face and thin head of hair. He studied the face, and through his mind ran all the faces he had interviewed, all the faces he had seen on the streets, all the faces he could possibly remember. He looked down at Harry's building and then onto the street—Orange Street. *Is it Pat Donolly?* Frank thought. *It looks like him from here. He lives on Orange Street.*

Pat Donolly had been an unemployed mill worker who took his carpentry skills and started his own business. It did well in the city and his business had been growing steadily. He now had two different crews working under him. *He's doing alright*, Frank thought in the rain. *It can't be him. Why would Pat Donolly want to kill himself? He just signed a big contract with the Irvings. Had to hire a dozen more workers for the job. A million-dollar project.*

Then Frank remembered that Pat Donolly had moved from the city to the Valley where he bought a big house by the yacht club. He remembered seeing it in the paper. Pat Donolly was a great rags to riches story and Frank had missed it and he remembered how disappointed he was for missing such a great story. No, it wasn't him.

"It's ready," the cameraman said.

Frank Beatrice looked through the camera and focused in on Harry's face. When he saw the face up close he took his eyes from the camera.

"Jesus Christ," he gasped.

"Who is it?"

"You know who that is?"

"No."

"It's Harry Cossaboom."

The cameraman was quiet.

"The bus driver who killed that kid in the summer," Frank said. "Grab the camera, we're going over there."

"But what about—"

"Forget that," he snapped. "Now come on."

***

Frank Beatrice and his cameraman rushed downstairs and across the street and up onto the roof of Harry's building.

Harry stood on the ledge holding his bottle of rum, the rain dripping from his clothes. Frank got the cameraman to stand behind him and follow him in slowly. He told him that if he screwed up he was never working with him again.

Harry turned around carefully when he heard them

behind him. He saw the cameraman on his knees with the camera and Frank Beatrice in front of him tucked under his umbrella.

"Mr. Cossaboom," Frank said calmly. "Mr. Cossaboom, do you know who I am?"

"Of course I do," Harry said and drank the last of his rum. He dropped the bottle and it bounced at Frank's feet but did not break.

"How are you?"

Harry glanced over his shoulder then turned back. "I've seen better days."

"I don't like the rain either," he said and glanced back at the camera. "So this is where you've been all this time."

Harry frowned.

"I never got to interview you," he continued. "I could have made you famous."

"I already was," Harry said.

Frank got a little closer.

"I can make you famous now," he smiled.

"What does it matter?" Harry asked.

"Nothing now," Frank answered. "But it will after you jump."

Harry wiped his eyes clear of rain.

"I don't think so."

"You should think about this, Mr. Cossaboom."

"Harry."

"You should think about this, Harry," Frank said quickly. "You should really take a minute and think about this."

"I jump and it's over," Harry said. "There isn't much to think about."

"But there is," he said. "There is much to think about. Have you ever heard of Ernest Hemingway?"

"No."

"He was the most famous writer of his time. *The Old Man and the Sea*?"

"I don't read much."

"Hemingway thought the way a man died was the most important part of his life," he went on. "So he committed suicide. Think about that for a second. You jump now, sure, you get what you want. Some little old lady sees you fall and calls the police. The ambulance comes, wraps you up and if you're lucky you get a nice little piece in the paper. But you're forgotten the next day and replaced by something or someone else."

"It's not that easy to forget," Harry said.

"But it is," he argued. "You think anyone remembers the name of that kid?"

"I do."

"But does anyone else?"

"His parents," he said. "And his friends."

"But that's all," Frank added. "Sure, everyone read the story. I can still remember the picture on the front page. But you think I remember his name?"

"Devon McGrady," he said.

"People will forget you," Frank continued. "Tomorrow you will be in the paper, sure. But you think anyone will give a fuck about you the day after that? You're gone as fast as you came. Just like the kid. You might as well never existed at all."

Harry lost his balance slightly, and Frank panicked and grabbed him by the arm.

"Why are you doing this?" Harry asked.

"It would make a great story," Frank answered honestly. "Think about it. We'll blow the whole thing up, do interviews, you'll be a star."

Harry did not move.

"I liked that story you did on that family a couple of years ago," Harry said. "They were from...where were they from?"

"Romania," Frank answered.

"Yes, Romania," he said. "And they took sanctuary in the church and the cops didn't come in and get them.

And all because they were in a church. A church is an odd building, don't you think? Gives you a certain kind of protection for no real reason other than because it's a church."

"Some people believe in a higher law."

"Do you?"

"Sure."

"Many do," Harry said. "They were there for quite a while."

"Over two weeks before they came out."

"And they were sent back to Romania."

"Yes," Frank said. "But they came back and they're living here now."

"It was a good story."

"I've done a lot of stories," he said. "Remember the Irving strike?"

"Which one?" Harry joked.

"The oil refinery, the long one."

"Of course I do," he said. "Everyone remembers that. I knew a guy who went back to work after six months. He was going to lose his house. They called him a scab. When they all went back they treated him so bad he quit. Poor bastard, didn't want to lose his house."

"I was there every morning at six o'clock," Frank said. "And I stood with them and interviewed them right up until it got settled."

"That was a long strike."

"It was hard work for me."

"What other stories do you remember?" Harry asked. The rain was starting to feel cold on him now and he shivered a bit and tucked his hands up into his sleeves.

"There are lots," he said. "But they're not all exciting. You don't want to know how many floods on Rothesay Avenue I've been to in the last ten years. Water up to my knees and standing in the rain just like this."

"Did you cover the explosion at the oil refinery?"

"Of course."

"What was the name of the guy who got killed?"

"I don't remember."

"I hope he wasn't forgotten," he said. "It's sad to hear of a working man dying at his job. Takes away from a good death."

"A good death is important."

"Yes it is."

"I can give you one. I can make you a star."

Harry took a moment, standing still. He was shivering now.

"A star."

"The biggest thing this city's ever seen."

"As big as Elsie?"

"Elsie?" Frank chuckled. "She's been out of the spotlight since she moved."

"But people will never forget her."

"People will never forget you," he said. "The name *Harry Cossaboom* will be legendary in this city."

"When could we do it?" Harry asked.

"No hurry if it's to be done right," he said. "It would be better on a sunny day. You could wait — a week or so. We'll do interviews, let the public get to know you, then the big show. People will never forget it."

Harry's eyes shot back at the camera then back at Frank who hovered under the umbrella.

"Can I have that umbrella?" he asked.

Frank handed him the umbrella. Harry held it over his head and he liked the sound of the rain hitting it. He liked seeing the rain fall around him and not into his eyes.

"I got that from Frank McKenna a few years ago," Frank said, squinting from the rain. "It's yours."

"Better on a sunny day."

"Much better," Frank smiled. "Nobody can see you in the rain. The camera work is messy. The whole thing would be better in good weather. You could see more on a clear day."

"Not on Saturday," Harry said without thought and

stepped down off the ledge, still holding the umbrella. He was unsteady on his feet. "Leafs game this Saturday."

Frank said nothing.

"Sunday," he continued. "How about Sunday?"

"Sunday's good," he said. "You got the whole Sabbath thing going. It could work."

"And I'll be a star."

"The biggest."

"And people will remember?"

"Do you see this?" Frank asked, pointing at the camera. "This incredible machine will make you immortal. They will never forget."

"It's important to be remembered," Harry said.

"Not too many people are," Frank said. "And you have a chance to be one of them."

Harry stood under the umbrella and thought of his grey apartment under him. He thought of his walls and of his bedroom and the rain hitting the window and dripping down. He thought of the bowling alley and Smitty. Then he thought of Catherine. Frank Beatrice stood patiently, the rain darkening his tie and soaking through his clothes.

Harry looked at Frank and swayed a bit on his feet. His eyes were half closed and glossed over. He held the umbrella casually so that the rain fell on his back.

"Can I ask you something?"

"Anything," Frank said.

"How did that writer kill himself?"

"He blew his head off with a shotgun."

"Hmm," Harry muttered; then, after thinking a moment, shook Frank's hand. "You think this will be a good story?"

"The best I've ever done," he said.

Harry smiled in the cold.

THREE

***

Frank Beatrice had found his masterpiece. On everyone's TV there he was with Harry, standing in the rain. They were both wet, and rain was dripping down the camera, blurring the vision, but it did not matter— the greatest event of the year could be seen live on TV.

"He's really gonna do it," a woman said, her eyes fixed on the screen. She was sitting on the edge of the couch, next to her husband.

"I've seen that guy somewhere," the husband frowned.

"He was the one who killed that kid on the bike in the summer," the wife said.

"The bus driver," he said. "Yes, I remember him now."

The wife turned to her husband.

"You think he's going to do it?"

"Frank Beatrice said he is."

"You really think?"

"Sure he is."

"I'm calling Sue to see if she's watching this."

She called her friend and she was watching it.

Immediately there was a buzz around the city and Harry's name was on everyone's lips. Frank Beatrice pushed every button he could and cashed in every favor owed to him. Harry was on the front page of Monday's *Evening Times Globe*. He had been interviewed by CBC radio on Tuesday. Tim Hortons on Rothesay Avenue had a neon sign that said **GO HARRY!** Soon all the Irving stores had signs with something about him, each with something different. One read: **HARRY COSSABOOM: SUPERSTAR**. Another read: **HARRY IS THE MAN**. And another: **HARRY WAS HERE**. Harry had even invaded the malls. McAllister Place had his picture in just about every store window.

"Yeah," the husband said again after his wife hung up the phone. "He'll do it."

"It's Sunday?"

"In the afternoon."

"You're working aren't you?"

"I'll call in sick," he said. "I'm not missing this."

***

Catherine was cautious coming out of the front doors of the school. It was icy and she had almost fallen in the morning. This time she made sure she wouldn't, now that the day was done. She took each step carefully but she was in a hurry and she slipped a little at the bottom, her boots slipping off the icy stone steps. She watched each step until she was solid on the salted sidewalk. She looked up and stopped suddenly.

There Harry was, leaning against a car with his arms crossed. He smiled the way he always had, a genuine, straight smile that lit a certain kind of pride upon his whole body. This was not a pretentious pride, but rather an innocent one, the kind Harry always comforted in having, much like that of a boy who scores a goal then sees his name in the paper the next day.

"I saw your picture in the paper today," Catherine said. "I have been trying to get hold of you since I heard in the staff room this morning. I called your house but there was no answer. I took a taxi to your place at lunch but you still weren't home. Oh, Harry, is it true?"

"It is," he smiled proudly.

"But you can't," she said. "This is your life and you're ending it. You can't do this Harry. This is all wrong. All terribly wrong."

"I thought you would be on my side," he frowned.

"I can't," she said. "Not for this. Not for this ever."

"You ended us," he said. "And I'm better now. I'm happy and we can be together again – if you want."

"Yes I want," she said. "I want it to be like it was before."

"Can it be that way again? Because that was good. Everything in us was good for a time."

Catherine wrapped her arms around him and held him tight, her hands squeezing the back of his coat.

"I don't know," she said, her face pressed into his shoulder. "Oh Harry, I'm glad you're happy but you can't do this."

"I'm happy," he said. "I'll read the books you give me. I'll even eat the food. This has nothing to do with us."

"Sunday you will be gone forever," she muttered. "I can't have you truly again, only for a few days. It has everything to do with us."

"Then we'll live a lifetime in these few days," he said.

"That sounds romantic," she said. "But it can't be done."

"Yes it can," he said. "We can do things, all kinds of things, anything you want."

"I want to have you here like this forever," she said. "Not for a few days. You can't be doing this. You can't do this to yourself."

"It's what I've always wanted."

"Is it?"

"Yes."

"But it's such a horrible thing," she said. "You are really going to kill yourself, truly honestly?"

"Yes," he said firmly. "Truly and honestly."

"I can't believe you're doing this."

"I'm going to be remembered," he said. "And that's

what makes me feel good inside. To know that I won't disappear alone."

"Everyone disappears alone," she said. "It's all an illusion."

"This is real," he said. "None of this is an illusion."

"Death is too real," she said. "Nobody is immortal."

"I am."

"No you're not."

"We'll see after Sunday if I'm still around."

"You can't do this."

"Did you read the article?" Harry grinned.

"I didn't need to," Catherine said. "You are all anyone talks about. And the students too. You know you're front page of the student paper? They think you're some kind of hero."

"Wonderful generation, isn't it?"

Catherine paused for a moment. "How are you, Harry?"

"I'm good," he smiled. "Honest. Everything is good now."

"That's good to see."

"Sunday I'll be better."

"I'm not letting you do this to yourself."

"It's my life," he said. "And I'm living it the way I want."

"You're not living it at all."

"Let's just forget about this now," Harry said. "I didn't come here to argue with you. We're done with all that. Do you want to go for a drive?"

"Whose car is that?" Catherine asked. She didn't want to think of it either.

"Mine for the week," he said. "Frank gave it to me."

"Frank Beatrice."

"He's a good guy. I can introduce you to him if you want."

"He's the reason for this. I hate him and I don't want to meet him."

"He's nothing like you think," Harry said. "He's very

nice. He works hard and he's a straight-up guy. I'm glad he's my friend."

"He is not your friend," Catherine said.

"Please can we forget about this for now?" Harry asked.

Catherine didn't answer.

"Do you want to go for a ride?" he asked again.

"Where?"

"Wherever you can drive."

"I can't drive."

"I'm here to teach you," he said. "Come on."

"You are crazy, Harry Cossaboom," she smiled. "Do you know that?"

"I'm hearing that a lot lately," he grinned.

"Does it bother you?"

"Nothing bothers me anymore," he said. "I don't have time for that. Now do you want to learn how to drive or not?"

"I'll crash."

"It's not my car."

"I could kill us both."

"We got snow banks for that," he shrugged. "They make good cushions."

Harry opened the car door. "I'll get us out of the city and you can go from there."

Catherine sat in the car.

Harry closed her door and walked around the front of the car. Catherine watched him through the windshield.

"I did a commercial for Irving today," he said as he buckled his seat belt. "It should be on TV sometime this week."

"That fast?"

"It's just a little clip of me getting gas," he said. "I smile and say how much I like Irving Oil. There's another shot of me at the counter buying Riverdale pop. They gave me a thousand dollars for an hour's work."

"But you don't even own a car," she said.

"Nobody knows that," he shrugged. "Besides, it's just TV. Wayne Gretzky's doing Folgers commercials. You can't tell me he needs the money. If it's good enough for him, it's good enough for me."

"Maybe he likes the coffee."

"Maybe," he said. "But he could buy all the coffee he wants. He doesn't need to do commercials. I bet he doesn't even drink it."

They drove across the Causeway, then to Grandview Avenue past the Industrial Park and behind the oil refinery.

"Frank covered the strike every day it was on," Harry said proudly. "He was there every morning at six o'clock."

Catherine didn't say anything.

"He was there for the explosion too."

He continued up Grandview Avenue, then down through Champlain Heights and onto Loch Lomond Road. He turned into Simonds High School and stopped the car in the empty parking lot.

"Your turn," he said and got out.

"I don't know about this," she said and climbed over the seat.

Harry opened the door and sat beside her.

"I can't reach the gas," she said.

"Pull the seat up."

Catherine yanked the seat so her jacket was pressed against the wheel.

"Put it in gear," Harry said.

Catherine looked at the gearshift between the seats.

"'D' for drive," he added softly.

Catherine found 'D'.

"Now give it some gas."

The car started forward. Catherine gripped the steering wheel with both hands. Her mouth hung open while the car went slowly along.

"Turn wherever you want," he said.

She turned up toward the the smaller parking lot in

front of the rink.

"I'm driving," she smiled like a little girl. "I'm driving!"

"I knew you could."

"I was always afraid of the other cars."

"You want to go on the street?"

"The parking lot is fine," she said. "One thing at a time."

"You're a good driver."

"Thank you."

"How does it feel?"

"It feels wonderful," she said smiling. "Truly wonderful."

"I'm glad you're happy," he said. "I'm sorry for the way I was."

"You're better now," she said. "And that's what matters."

"I'm sorry."

Catherine stopped the car. She hit the brakes hard and their seat belts locked.

"Touchy brakes."

"I love you, Catherine."

"Oh Harry," she said. "I love you. Don't let us be like that again."

"I'm better now," he said. "Everything is better now."

He leaned across the seat and kissed her. Catherine put her arm on Harry's shoulder. The car started forward and Harry quickly found 'P' without looking.

"Are you worried about Sunday?" Catherine asked.

"No."

"You're not worried at all?"

"Sunday I live forever," he said. "How can you worry about that?"

"You're famous now."

"Yes."

"I don't want you to die."

"I'm not going to die."

"But you are."

"Everyone dies."

"In time, yes," Catherine said. "Everyone dies. That's why it's what you do in your own time that's important. Not after you die. You can't feel anything. Or know anything, or love anything."

"I think you're wrong."

"How can you think that?"

"Because I know I won't be gone after Sunday," he answered. "I'll be here forever."

"Your name will be here but you won't."

"Nothing you can say or do will change this," he said. "It feels right to me. It feels good to me. For the first time in as long as I can remember I feel alive. Really alive."

"I hope it feels good."

"It does," he said. "It feels the same way you did the moment you realized you were driving."

"That felt good."

"Yes."

"And you're happy?" Catherine asked.

"Very."

"I'm happy too then."

"You're just saying that."

"I'm happy for you," she said. "I'm too sad to be happy for me."

"Are you hungry?"

"No."

"It's supper time and you've worked all day. You must be hungry."

"I'm not."

"Please Catherine," he said. "Can we be together like we were before? Can we be that way again, even if it's only for a few days? Can you try for me at least?"

Catherine thought a moment.

"I'm sorry, but it's hard."

"I know."

"It's so hard I can't stop thinking of it," she said. "But I'll try, for you."

Harry leaned over and kissed her.

"Are you hungry?" he asked again.

"A little."

"Where do you want to go?"

"It doesn't matter."

"But it does," he smiled. "I have all kinds of money. We can eat anywhere now."

"I don't like expensive restaurants," she said.

"Pick a place."

"Don Cherry's is good."

"Sounds good to me," he said. "Do you want to drive?"

"I don't think so."

"You might surprise yourself."

"Not in a good way," she said. "I'll run us right off the road."

***

Harry parked down on Water Street behind Chizzlers and they walked to Market Square in the cold. The wind is colder down by the water. It comes in from the river and blows along the Boardwalk. Catherine shivered and Harry put his arm around her and held her tight, the snow blowing up into his face.

Once inside Market Square, Harry noticed his picture in the window of a craft shop that was already closed. Catherine was unbuttoning her coat and didn't see the picture. Don Cherry's was busy and they had to wait a few minutes at the front before being seated. Heads turned and caught glimpses of Harry while they stood. They were seated by the windows that looked down onto the Boardwalk and they could see the snow whirling, sparkling white outside.

"It's nice looking out onto the cold when you're in a warm place," Catherine said. "It makes you appreciate the warmth."

Harry held his menu and looked out the window. "It

doesn't make me any warmer," he said. "It sure is blowing out there."

A waiter came and took their drink orders.

"I saw people looking at you at the door," she said. "Everyone knows who you are."

Harry enjoyed the attention but kept it to himself. He didn't want to make Catherine sad again.

"Did you do something to your hair?" he asked.

"I colored it last week," she said. "You didn't notice it?"

"I didn't notice anything last week. I'm sorry for that. For all of that."

"It's done," Catherine remarked. "And let's forget about it."

"I'm truly sorry," Harry said again.

"We are past that now."

"Am I wrong wanting this?"

"No," she said. "I don't think you're wrong in wanting to be happy. That's all everyone wants. You're just going about it the wrong way. Does it feel wrong?"

"I don't know how it feels," he said. "All I know is that I'm happy and I have been down too long to let it go."

"Then hold onto it," she said. It hurt her inside when she heard herself say it.

"It's good to be dedicated to something."

"Yes it is," she smiled.

The waiter came over with a bottle of champagne and two glasses.

"The couple in the corner asked me to bring you this," he said and popped open the bottle.

Harry twisted himself around. There in the corner under a big picture of Steve Yzerman holding the Stanley Cup was a young couple, much younger than Harry and Catherine. Harry waved at them and raised his glass and drank. The couple grinned excitedly.

"That was nice of them," Catherine said. "Should we buy them a drink?"

"I don't know," Harry frowned. "Is that what you do? I

suppose it wouldn't hurt if we did."

Harry called the waiter over and ordered the same thing for the couple.

"They look so happy," she sighed. "Do you think we look as happy as them?"

"It's nice to think so."

"Yes it is."

An old lady, slow in her motions, approached their table as they spoke. She had an innocent face with sad eyes that made you feel bad that she was old and you were not.

"I'm so very sorry to interrupt you," she began, her voice soft and sweet. "Mr. Cossaboom, sir, would you mind signing an autograph for my grandson? You are all he talks about."

Harry looked at Catherine, then back to the little old lady. "I would be happy to," he said. The old lady gave him a pen and Harry signed his napkin. "You tell your grandson that this is the first autograph I have ever signed."

"I most certainly will," she said in an old lady exaggerated gasp. "I most certainly will indeed. Thank you so very much, Mr. Cossaboom. He is not going to believe it."

"You're welcome," Harry said politely.

The old lady folded the napkin and put it in the pocket of her sweater, smiled at Harry, then to Catherine, then walked back to her table.

"That was weird," he said.

"Did it feel good?" Catherine asked, not wanting an answer.

"Like learning to drive," he smiled.

***

By Wednesday, Harry Cossaboom T-shirts were being sold.

Harry's next commercial was for Chizzlers on Prince William Street. He stood beside the owner, Big Johnnie Sebastian, wearing a Chizzlers cap. The director, Francis Kettle, had Harry smiling and eating a steak. Chizzlers had a big screen TV upstairs and was airing the jump with ten-cent wings, *with the purchase of any pitcher from five fine selections of draft, including Moosehead, Alpine, Keith's, Canadian, and Blue.*

I always eat my steak here, Harry said, smiling wide. *And the prices can't be beat!*

That's right. Here at Chizzlers it's a way of life! Come join us Sunday and watch Harry on the big screen, the way it's supposed to be watched.

Can I watch it here too, Big Johnnie?

Don't be foolish Harry. You're the star!

Oh yeah!

Ha ha ha!

Chizzlers, 212 Prince William Street, where everyday is a way of life.

"Good good," Mr. Kettle said from behind his camera. "That's all we need, Mr. Sebastian. And thank you Mr. Cossaboom, very well done."

"When will it air?" Harry asked.

"I will edit this afternoon," Mr. Kettle said. "It should be on television sometime in a few days if Mr. Sebastian settles the final edit000."

"I need this on TV as fast as you can get it," Big Johnnie said. "Harry jumps this Sunday. That only gives me three days to advertise. I trust your judgement, Mr. Kettle. I know what you have done with Mel's Shoe Palace. You get it done as soon as you can. I need it on the air."

Mr. Kettle nodded, then turned to Harry.

"Mr. Cossaboom," he said. "I will see you this afternoon at Mel's."

"Yes," Harry said, looking at his watch. "I hope it goes as quickly as this one."

"I have seen the script," Mr. Kettle added. "It shouldn't take long."

"How much is Mel Quigley paying you?" Big Johnnie asked Harry.

"I can't say," he said. "But it's enough. And you have paid me enough."

"You come in here tonight," he said. "Anything you want is free. Bring your friends and have some drinks, eat something, have a few more drinks. It's all on me. Tonight is your night, my friend. Anything you want, you got it."

Harry shook Big Johnnie's hand. "I'll be here," he said. "Absolutely."

"And you too," Big Johnnie pointed at Catherine who was standing in the back behind Mr. Kettle and a lighting man. "I should expect to see you here too."

"It sounds like fun," Catherine smiled.

Harry took her by the hand. "I'll see you this afternoon," he said to Mr. Kettle. Then, turning to Big Johnnie: "See you tonight."

It was early in the day and the sun had not yet shined on Prince William Street. Harry shivered in the cold as he and Catherine walked to the car, parked down on Water Street, a few spots up from where they parked the night before.

"Big Johnnie paid me more than Mel Quigley," Harry said. "Both commercials are fast and cheap but I'm making money doing nothing. Irving was the cheapest but I expected that — and I still got a thousand bucks."

"Maybe if you had a car they would have paid more," Catherine said.

"Maybe," he said. "It's weird selling yourself like this."

"You're a star."

"I'm a money-maker," he said. "But I'm making money too so I shouldn't be upset."

"Are you upset?" she quickly asked.

"I don't know," he said. "No, I don't think so. No, of course not. I'm very happy."

Catherine could not look at Harry directly. "That's good."

"Yes it is," he muttered. "It's good to be happy. I'm doing this because it makes me happy. People do things to make them happy all the time. Isn't that what you said?"

"I think so," she said. "I do things because they make me feel good."

"And that's why I'm doing all this," he said. "I'm happy doing it. It makes me feel good. And Sunday will make me feel good too."

"I hope so."

"Do you think it won't?"

"If it makes you happy, it's the right thing," Catherine said dryly.

"It does."

She paused. "Then it is."

"Yes," Harry shivered. "Yes, it must be the right thing."

Mel's Shoe Palace gave Harry five thousand dollars for wearing a pair of Mel's sneakers on Sunday. And there was Mel, smiling that famous smile that sold itself in every Saint Johner's living room. And Mel's girls too, singing and dancing behind him.

They say: Hey Mel, hey Mel, why you got the blues?
I say: Hey girls, hey girls, cause I got no shoes.
I got no shoes and I got the blues,
I got no shoes and I want to play,
Mel's Shoe Palace—low prices everyday!
Mel's Shoe Palace
Mel's Shoe Palace
The place your feet like to meet!

Hey everyone, your ol'pal Mel here, from Mel's Shoe Palace. Want the best shoes for the lowest price? Want the best service in Saint John? Then come on in to Mel's, where we got it all—sneakers, walkers, hikers, boots, sandals, pumps—
if you can put it on your feet, then we got it. Come on in and say hello. Harry Cossaboom does. Tell them Harry:
I buy all my shoes at Mel's Shoe Palace. It's the place where your feet like to meet.
1299 Rothesay Avenue (across from Burger King)
Open seven days a week.

***

"I'm tired and it's not even suppertime," Harry said to Catherine as they drove back to his apartment. "I know those commercials don't look like much but they still require effort. It's not easy to smile all the time."

"But they pay you for it," Catherine said.

"And I smile," he said. "I smile and I smile and they give me money for it, I know."

"You have a nice smile."

"Is it worth so much money?"

"It is to them."

"Is it to you?"

"Yes," she assured him. "I would pay if you didn't give it to me for free."

"I like to smile for you," he said. "My smiles for you are real. I would never make you pay."

"That's a good thing," she said. "Because I couldn't afford it."

"You don't make anything from my smile," he said as he drove. "And you still want it. That's why I would always give it to you."

"I love you, Harry."

Harry stopped the car and kissed Catherine.

"Kiss me again," she said.

He studied her face for a moment.

"Why do you love me, Catherine?"

"Because I do."

He smiled sadly.

"That's a good answer."

"It's the truth," she said. "You make me very happy."

"We make each other happy," he said. "We're pretty good together."

"Yes we are," she said. "I'm happy."

"Good."

"Are you truly happy, Harry?"

"Of course."

"I don't think you are."

"What makes you say that?"

"I may be wrong."

"I think you are," he said. "My life is good right now. I have everything I want."

"I'm sorry," she said. "I won't say it again."

"Tell me why."

"I may be wrong."

"Tell me."

"That night in Mispec," she said. "When you spoke of your dream; when you spoke of the bus service with Nick; of wanting to be like Elsie, I saw something in you, like a shine. It was in your eyes and in your words. You were so passionate and everything you said had meaning, like you were going to get it no matter what it took. That's when I fell in love with you."

Harry listened intently as Catherine continued.

"And now you have everything," she said. "You have everything you wanted—you're more famous now than you ever dreamed. But I don't see the shine I saw before. I don't see it anywhere."

They sat quiet for a short while.

"Do you want to go again?" Harry asked. "It's a good place to talk."

"Where?"

"Mispec."

"Now?"

"Now."

"I thought you were tired."

"I am," he said. "But I'd like to go."

"It will be too cold."

"We'll stay in the car and watch the waves," he said.

"I like the waves."

"Then let's go."

By the time they arrived at Mispec, the sky was dark and they could only see the blackness of the water down on the beach and the grey rippling of the waves as they broke on shore. There were no ships in the harbour but it was a clear night and they could see the stars in the sky bright and clear.

"Do you see the Big Dipper?" Harry asked, leaning in against the steering wheel and looking up through the windshield.

Catherine leaned forward.

"I see it," she said.

"Do you see the tail?"

"Yes."

"The two last stars on the tail, they make a line. Do you see it?"

Catherine took a moment.

"Yes."

"Take that line down, and the one that lines up with it is the North Star," he said. "You can always tell it from there. From there you can tell time. When they are lined up perfectly it's midnight."

Then Harry sat back in his seat with a puzzled look.

"I think that's right," he said. Then leaning forward once again, "Yes, that's right. The North Star is the one all other stars circle. From there you can tell time, using that star and lining it up with others. The tail on the Big Dipper, when it lines up perfectly straight, that's when you know it's midnight. If you can see it now you can tell it's not lined up."

"I see it," she said.

"We should come at midnight and I can show you."

"I would like that," she smiled, her head still tilted upward, looking through the windshield. "Where do you think Heaven is?"

"It's not up there," Harry answered dryly.

"Where is it then?"

"I don't think there is."

"You don't believe in Heaven?" Catherine frowned, sitting back in her seat.

"After the accident I wanted to believe – tried to believe – there was a Heaven and that Devon McGrady was there," he said. "That he went somewhere good. But I was fighting myself and it didn't feel right. I just knew he was nowhere and nothing, under the ground dead. I hurts the most when I think of that. But it feels true to me."

Harry scratched his forehead as he sat still, his head straight and his eyes in a blank stare. Catherine remained quiet and listened.

"It hurts terrible though," he said after a moment. "Like something in me is twisting and knotting my insides and it does nothing but ache and hurt and I try not to think of it but there he is. His face I remember perfectly, like he's right there in front of me. But I still can't remember that second when I hit him. It comes to me in pieces in dreams but I lose it before I can remember. Sometimes I wake up with the twisting and aching though. That's when I know I remembered."

"You should talk to someone," Catherine said.

"There's no sense now."

"So this is the reason for what you're doing," she said sitting up.

"No," he said firmly. "It's to live. I have told you that already."

"Do you believe in God?"

"No."

"I didn't think you did. How can you believe in God and not Heaven?"

"You can believe in anything you want," he said. "A God and no Heaven maybe."

"So you do believe in God."

"No," he said. "Who made God if God made everything?"

Catherine fell back into her seat and sighed.

"And if there is a God, what has he done for me?" he continued. "What has God done for anyone? We get the sun one day and it rains the next. You watch the news and all you see is hate and killing and death. If there is a God, I'm sure he'd have more control of things. No kids dying in the street from cars and busses."

"But there is a lot of good in the world too."

"Not very much."

"There is hope and freedom and love."

"Yes, there is love."

"We have love."

"Yes we do," Harry smiled. "But I don't think it's because of God. I love you because I love you."

"I love you so very much," she said, tears coming into her eyes.

"Do you believe you love me because of God?"

"I don't know," she said. "Maybe. If God made me and you then I suppose, yes, I love you because of God."

"God has no place between us," he said.

"Why not?"

"God has no place in love, in anyone's love. Besides, I don't think he exists. If he did, there would be no hate in the world. And no war and no suffering and no death."

"What about Jesus?"

"He was an incredible man," he said. "There's no doubt about it – the most famous man who ever lived. I would never be as famous as him."

"You're not Jesus."

"No, I'm not," he said. "But I'm not much different."

"Do you believe in death?"

"Of course I do." He paused for a second. "But I've found a way around it."

Catherine looked up through the windshield once again.

"Look at these stars," she sighed. She did not want to hear Harry speak any more of Sunday. "They're beautiful. Who do you think made them?"

"Not God," he said dryly. "They're too beautiful. There's too much peace in them to be made by God."

"It sounds to me like you believe in him," she said. "You just don't like him."

"I believe something made the stars and the sky."

"Why not God?"

"It's too simple. I don't think there's only one guy running the whole show. Sure, it's a good story, but too simple to handle this grand universe. Things are never that simple."

"Listen to you," Catherine said. "That doesn't sound like you. Talking of no God and grand universes."

"Does it bother you?"

"No," she said. "Well yes, a little I guess. But not in a bad way. Not in a bad way at all. I'm just surprised to hear you say that. Have you always thought this way? I think it would be a lonely way to live."

"You are always alone," Harry said. "In any religion. You can gather in groups of hundreds or thousands or even millions and still at the end of it all, you are alone."

"You're talking about when you die."

"Yes," he said. "Isn't that what religion is for? To help you deal with death?"

"Perhaps," she answered reluctantly.

"That's what it's for."

"But you have no religion at all."

"It doesn't matter."

Catherine crossed her arms. "It surprises me," she said again.

"When I was a boy my mother used to drag me to church every Sunday. She used to get all dressed up fancy. Nothing simple about Sundays with my mother. She would make sure I wore a tie. I was twelve years old. And the tie, she always made sure, was tight and straight and that not a hair on my head was out of place. If I had food on my mouth she would lick her finger and wipe it off."

Harry smiled, then, relaxed, and resting his head back on the seat, chuckled to himself.

"She was quite a lady," he said. "Nothing simple about her. She wore my grandmother's brooch – a big shiny gold thing and I remember how it shined in the church. I don't think there was ever a time when I believed in any of it, though. Not even as a boy. But I believed in that brooch my mother wore. I believed in that. When she died she left it to me. It's at home in my drawer."

"What did you believe?"

"I thought she was God."

"I would like to see it," Catherine said.

"It's really quite ugly when you look at it now," he smiled, a straight, lazy smile. "But when I was a boy I used to think it was a treasure, like something a queen would wear. My father used to tell her it made her look like a fairy tale. He never went to church. My mother would ask him once and that was all."

"Was he religious?"

"I don't know," he said. "I don't think so. He was a straightforward guy. Like me, I guess. I think he needed more to convince him too."

"When did he die?"

"Two years ago. Heart attack."

"I'm sorry."

"Don't be," he said. "He was an old man. My mother died when I was young. She was young too, younger than I am now. But I always see her as older. Funny how time works, isn't it?"

And Harry looked back up to the stars and sat quiet for a moment.

"My father used to swear around the house," he grinned. "And my mother would bless him and bless the house and sometimes me if she thought I heard what he said. I'm sure my mother spent most of her time in confession for my father."

Harry sat with a smile.

"I believe in God," Catherine said.

"You would make a good mother," he said.

"I have always believed in God."

"You don't go to church."

"I used to but I stopped."

"Why did you stop?"

"I just did," she said. "I don't know. Sometimes I see Father Patrick in the market and he says hello. I feel bad when I see him because he knows I've stopped going. But he still says hello and he still smiles. You should talk to him."

"To a priest?" he frowned. "Why?"

"He might be able to answer some of your questions," she said.

"I don't have any questions."

"None?"

"No."

"Will you talk to him?" she asked. "I can go and see him and tell him about you. I'll go tomorrow."

Harry sighed, then turned to Catherine.

"Would it make you happy if I saw him?"

Catherine smiled.

"Very much," she said. "He's young. I think you would like him."

"He won't convince me of anything."

"He won't try. He'll just listen."

"One talk won't make me believe," he said. "But if it makes you happy then I'll go."

"I'm not trying to make you believe," Catherine said.

"I'm not trying to change you in any way. You're you and I love you as you. I like our differences. But I still believe. If there is no God then I have nothing to lose. If there is, I lose everything."

"If there's a God and I meet him, he'll appreciate that I've been honest with myself. That should be enough to get me in," Harry said. "He can't afford to be too strict these days. Otherwise it'd be an empty place."

"There is Hell," Catherine said.

"Then it must be the place to go," he said. "Make sure there is sun tan lotion in my casket."

"Don't joke of that."

"Alright, alright," he grinned. "But if there's a Heaven, and if there's a Hell, send me South because I won't know anyone North."

"Your mother."

"Yes," he said. "If there's a Heaven she's there."

"And your father."

"No," he said very seriously now. "Only my mother."

Harry's seriousness caused a minute of silence to pass between them.

"I like hearing stories of when you were young," Catherine smiled. "Tell me more."

"I can't think of any right now," Harry shrugged.

"When you do will you tell me?"

"I will," he said. "But not now. I'm too tired. Let's go home. I need some sleep before we go out tonight."

***

Chizzlers was smoky and crowded to the elbows. The music was loud. Harry was sitting at a table with Catherine and Nick. He was feeling good, the music vibrating off his chest as he watched the small dance floor and the colored lights shining off and on to the music. Nick was also drunk and he smiled at Harry now and then, drinking his beer, then motioning to the wait-ress (who was there to serve Harry's table alone, Big Johnnie had told him when they arrived) to bring him another. Catherine had been sipping gin but did not seem as drunk as Harry and Nick, who tapped their hands on the table or their laps, turning their heads at the women like high school kids drunk in a bar for the first time and eager to get laid.

"I'm hungry," Harry said.

"Me too," Nick added.

"Anything we want is ours," Harry smiled. "Are you hungry Catherine?"

"No."

"I want a steak," Nick said. "Like the one you told me about."

"Good good," he smiled again. "Where is the wait-ress? I'll get us two of those and more beer."

Catherine placed her empty glass on the table.

"Do you want another gin?" Harry asked.

"I would like wine this time," she said.

"Yes!" Nick cried, holding his beer in the air.

"Where is that waitress?" Harry frowned, popping his head up.

"No tip for her," Nick said.

"Not if she doesn't get here soon," Harry said seri-ously. "She's only got us to serve."

"Maybe she is serving someone else," Catherine said.

"She better not be."

Nick leaned in to Harry with a big grin on his face. "I feel there is a traitor among us; that one of you will de-ceive me."

Harry smiled. "She better get here soon."

"I'll go," Catherine said.

"No," Harry snapped. "You sit."

"I can get us drinks. You get your food," she said. "She has spoiled you tonight."

Catherine got up from the table and made her way

through the crowd to the bar. A young woman, drunken, stumbled to their table and sat herself in Catherine's seat. She had long blonde hair, pretty dark eyes and innocent little teeth that showed white when she smiled.

"Mr. Cossaboom," she said. "Can I have your autograph?"

Harry smiled at Nick.

"Of course."

The young woman leaned in close to Harry and opened her shirt, showing her breasts. He looked at Nick again and smiled.

"Sign it anywhere," she said, handing him a black marker she said she got from the bar.

Harry signed his name across the top of her chest. The woman leaned in close to him again, handing him a folded piece of paper.

"You call me before Sunday," she said. "You can sign anything you want."

Nick was listening but did not hear. Harry sat back as the woman kissed him on the cheek and stumbled back into the crowd. Nick's mouth hung open.

"How old do you think?"

"Twenty, maybe," Harry said.

Nick smiled wide.

Four young men, hair slicked and spiked hard, came to the table. One of them was wearing a T-shirt that said: HARRY WAS HERE and Harry signed it for him. He signed autographs for all of them. Another drunken woman came and Harry signed another.

"Frank told me to expect this," he said.

"It's crazy," Nick added. "They all want a piece of you. The whole city does."

"It sure feels like it tonight."

"I saw Frank Beatrice on TV last night," Nick said. "He said he is thinking about taking a job in Toronto when this is all done."

"He never told me that."

"For the CBC," Nick continued. "He got an offer for the national news. I heard he's been getting offers from the States too. More money there."

"He never mentioned it."

"Do you think he'll go?"

"I don't know," Harry said.

"He's become a star too," Nick said. "You took him into the national spotlight."

"I hope he doesn't leave. He's good for Saint John."

"He won't stay," Nick said. "Not if there's an offer somewhere else. He'll get out if he can."

"I hope not," Harry muttered.

Catherine came back to the table with a bottle of white wine and three glasses. She filled each glass and sat down.

"A toast!" Nick announced, holding his glass high. Harry and Catherine held up their glasses. "To the making of Harry Cossaboom."

"To the making of Harry Cossaboom," Harry smiled drunkenly as their glasses dinged together. Catherine was saddened as she drank.

A flash went off and the three of them turned in surprise. Harry recognized the photographer from the *Evening Times Globe* who had taken the picture that was on the front page of Monday's paper (and everyday since).

"One more," the photographer said. "Can you look this way with your glasses in the air?"

"This is my time," Harry said. "I'm here with my friends."

"Just one, Mr. Cossaboom," he pleaded. "One and I will leave you alone."

Harry sighed and lifted his glass.

Nick took a cab home at the end of the night. Harry and Catherine walked home in the dark. Harry's wrist was sore from signing autographs.

"It's becoming a fashion," he said, rubbing his wrists.

"What is?" Catherine frowned.

"Me," he said.

"Isn't that what you wanted?"

"I want to be remembered."

"And you will," she said. "You will be remembered forever."

"Do you think they'll name a street after me?"

"They might."

"Harry Cossaboom Road," he said, stumbling along. "That would be nice."

"I would drive on it," she said.

"It would be a two-way street."

"I'll learn."

"Will you remember me, Catherine?"

Catherine stopped and faced Harry.

"I will never forget you," she said. "Ever."

"Because I want you to remember me."

"I love you, Harry."

"I love you," he said, then kissed her softly on the lips. "Of all the people who remember me in this city, I want you to the most."

"I will," she said. "Oh Harry, I will never forget."

"Will people forget Frank Beatrice if he leaves?"

"I don't know."

"I think they will," he said. "I think they will if he betrays them by leaving."

"Why do you say that?"

"Because he doesn't care about this city. He doesn't care what happens to it after I've gone. Nick told me he read an article that said Frank was leaving after Sunday."

"I read it," Catherine said.

"Do you think he will leave?"

"I think he will."

"It's my fault," Harry frowned. "People will know that I was the reason Frank Beatrice left. They won't forget that. And they'll hate me."

"They will not," she said. "If Frank Beatrice leaves, it's by his own doing. He's a man who makes his own decisions and people know that."

"Yes," he said. "I suppose he is. But I will be his final story in Saint John."

"People love you, Harry," she said.

"It isn't what I expected."

"How do you mean?"

"It just isn't."

"Then quit it," she said enthusiastically. "Quit it all right now and we can be together every day."

"I won't have a street."

"I don't want a street," she said. "I want you."

"You are a good and dear woman," Harry said. "I'm going to miss you."

"Don't talk of that please," she said. "Don't talk of it ever again. Please let's just forget it. I'm trying to be happy for you but it's hard. It's the hardest thing I've ever done."

"You are a dear sweet thing," he said and kissed her.

"You don't have to do this," she said, tears coming into her eyes. "You can drop it all right now."

"Stop it."

"Do you believe in this moment?" she persisted. "Do you believe in me here right now?"

"Yes," he answered.

"Do you?"

"I said yes."

"Then why are you doing this to yourself?"

Harry stepped back and held Catherine by both shoulders. "I have found a way to go beyond the now," he said. "Can't you see that? I can go into tomorrow."

"But you're wrong," Catherine said. She took a breath. She had tried over and over, and it seemed everything she said now was all the same. "You can't do that. It's impossible. Your memory will go on and that's all. What is important is how it goes today; and how it goes into the evening. Tomorrow is secondary."

"Secondary?" he frowned.

"It never comes," she said. She turned to the street and pointed. "Do you see that sign?"

Harry turned and saw the Charlotte Street sign.

"Who is Charlotte?" she asked. "Do you know?"

"No."

"Have you ever looked at that sign and thought who it was?"

"No."

He had seen the sign a million times.

"Then how do you believe Harry Cossaboom Street will be any different?" she said. "And that's if they name a street after you."

"You'll know," he said.

"I can know you now," she said quickly. "Today. Right now— it's always here. It never goes away. Here and now where I can hold you and feel you and love you."

"People will know," Harry said. "Everyone will know me like they know me now. I bet people in Toronto know who I am, people who never knew I existed before this week. They're looking at us for once. They're the ones on the outside looking in."

Catherine wiped her eyes but the tears kept falling.

"Why are you doing this to me?" she wept.

Harry didn't answer.

"Then let's just forget about Sunday and we can be together now, forever."

Harry wrapped his arm around her as she cried. He was very drunk and in his head he thought of Charlotte Street and wondered who Charlotte was.

***

Harry did not leave his apartment all day Thursday. It

was a dark day but he was bothered by the morning light when he got up to get a drink of water. He was very thirsty, his lips dry and his tongue sticking to the top of his mouth. He went into the kitchen and drank four glasses of tapwater, drinking them down in one breath, each glass a little colder than the previous. Catherine had already gone to work but he did not hear her leave. He went back to his room and threw a towel over the curtains. The room darkened a little and he fell back into bed, his belly swollen from the water.

Harry slept long and deep, not once moving until he opened his eyes and saw the alarm clock. – 3:22. He stretched out in bed then relaxed, breathing smoothly through his nose. His mouth was dry once again. Look-ing at the window, he saw the towel hanging crooked, pressing the curtains up against the glass. The walls, he noticed as he lay, were dreary and plain and gave him a sad feeling in his stomach. They looked especially pale with the towel darkening all the room. He was sad too because the day was almost done, and he knew it had been a grey and dirty day while he slept. He was still in bed when Catherine came. She went into the bedroom and sat on the side of the bed.

"It usually feels good to only have one day left in the week," she said. "But today it feels awful. It feels so bad I don't know how to say it. It feels horribly awful."

Harry sat up in bed.

"Don't be sad," he said. "Please don't be sad."

"I can't help it," she said. "The week is ending. It went so fast."

Harry said nothing, then:

"I have another story for you. From when I was a boy."

Catherine wiped her eyes.

"Tell me," she said.

Harry adjusted himself in bed again.

"My father grew up in Sussex," he began. "On a farm. He was never a city boy like me. He met my mother in

the city and he stayed for her. But he loved the country
and he left the city as often as he could. I remember the
fishing trips we used to go on. He would take me salmon
fishing in the Mirimachi. I can still remember him holding
the branches back when we hiked along the river."

Catherine smiled a sad sort of smile when she thought
of Harry as a boy, and his father holding the branches
back.

"Sometimes my uncle would meet us there," he continued. "We used to sleep in the back of his truck. In the
morning we would fry bacon and eggs on a Coleman
stove and I loved the smell of the propane. At night, after
spending the whole day fishing, we would fry what we
caught and eat it with bread. Those were the best meals.
My father wasn't religious, but he was when he was in
the woods. There was something about the forest that
made him spiritual. My uncle would go on up river and
fish alone, leaving my father and me together. We would
find a good pool of water, a dark pool where the salmon
were. My father always knew where the best spots were.
When he caught a fish, he would hide it in the rocks
where we stood so that if someone else came by they
wouldn't think it was a good place to fish."

"I have never gone fishing," Catherine said.

"I haven't been in ten years," he said. "Not since he
got too old to go into the woods."

"Tell me more."

"When we slept I used to hear the river down over the
bank," he said. "And in the mornings when it was light the
river was louder, as if it had new energy first thing in the
morning, like it had slept all night. When Sunday came it
was time to head back to Saint John. My uncle would
drive behind us through miles and miles of dirt roads, all
through the woods, until it was time to go our separate
ways. He would pull up beside us and my father would
roll down his window. They would talk for a minute or two.
Then my uncle went one way and we went the other. I

can still remember how sad I used to feel when he pulled away. It was then that I knew the fishing trip was over."

He took Catherine's hand.

"I'm sad too," he said. "I'm sad because our week is almost over. And I'm sorry for making you sad."

Catherine started to cry and she hugged him, crying into his shoulder.

Harry stayed in Friday as well, until a limo came and drove him and Nick to Harbour Station, where they had ringside seats to the WWF. It was a sold out show, and in the middle of the event, a light shined on Harry and he stood for the crowd and received a standing ovation. Harry waved and the crowd cheered. Even the wrestlers clapped their hands.

They met all the wrestlers after the show. They went down into their dressing rooms and Harry signed autographs for them; all well-known men, millionaires and superstars to kids and full-grown men alike, and all of them wanting their pictures taken with Harry Cossaboom. Harry signed for them all, but to him they were the stars and he went home with his own pictures.

FOUR

***

"Bring your camera," a young girl said to her twin sister as they sat in front of the TV. "Don't forget—you'll need a couple rolls of film. If we can get close enough, we'll get some good shots of him just before he jumps."

"We could sell them," the sister said. "We could. There's bound to be a book after the whole thing and I bet they'll need pictures."

***

On the other side of the city, two teenaged boys sat in a bedroom flicking channels. They were bored but it was too cold and too wet for pond hockey or anything else outside. In the room they were warm and dry. They saw Harry on TV.

"We'll be the first ones on Orange Street tomorrow morning," one said. "We'll get up early and go down there so that we're in the front."

"We should camp out tonight," the other boy suggested.

"We'll freeze."

"We won't get to the front if we don't."

The boy thought very briefly. Then with eyes wide open he turned.

"Do you want to?"

"I want to be in the front."

"I'll say I'm going to your house for the night," he said. "And you say you're at mine."

The two boys sat in the warmth of the bedroom anticipating nightfall. By mid-afternoon the day warmed a little but by suppertime the cold came on again, and the city was empty not long after dark. Harry's Irving commercials ran all day and into the night, along with the Chizzlers and Mel's Shoe Palace ads. And there was Mel Quigley, standing beside Harry with a smile, matching Big Johnnie Sebastian's at Chizzlers.

They say: Hey Mel, hey Mel, why you got the blues?
I say: Hey girls, hey girls, 'cause I got no shoes…

***

Harry awoke at eight o'clock Saturday morning. His apartment was well lit and the sun came into his window and warmed the spot where he lay. He felt fresh and alive as he stretched his arms out wide across the bed and yawned. He looked out his window and saw the blue of the sky, not a cloud. The blueness made him feel good and he smiled and lit a cigarette. Catherine rolled over and kissed him on the cheek as he smoked. She had decided, as she did every morning when she woke, to support Harry, and to be there beside him. But every day she could not do it without feeling a hole in her stomach, deep and aching when she thought of how time was running out.

"Tomorrow is the big day," she whispered.

"Yes," Harry said. "That's what I'm thinking."

"And does it still feel good?"

"Yes. I hope the weather is right," he said. "I hope it's clear like today."

"It will be a good day no matter what," she said. "It's your day."

"It is my day," he smiled. "Isn't it?"

"The whole day is yours."

"They could name a day after me," he smiled again. "That wouldn't be too bad. I would be remembered for it. Maybe make it a holiday."

"It would be my favorite holiday."

"Better than Christmas?"

"Much better."

"I suppose," he said. "It would be better to celebrate a holiday for someone you actually knew."

Catherine rolled back over and sank her head into her pillow. She cried into the pillow but Harry didn't notice. When he finished his cigarette, he went to the living room and looked out his window and down onto the street.

The snow was wet in the morning air and the sidewalks shined with water. A thin stream of water ran alongside the street by the sidewalk. He opened the window and the air was cool but not cold. He took in a breath and hung his head out. Directly below, a camera flashed. Then another. He looked down and saw a small crowd gathered at the base of his building.

"Give us a smile Harry!" one man cried, his voice echoing up.

Harry smiled and waved and a stream of flashes went off. Passersby stopped and joined the crowd and soon a mob of people flooded the street to get a glimpse of Harry Cossaboom. Cars stopped and heads popped out windows and looked up.

"How do you feel, Harry?" a woman yelled.

"I feel great," he said from his window. "Look at this beautiful day."

"Are you looking forward to tomorrow?" another voice cried.

"It couldn't come soon enough," he said.

He smiled and waved once more to the crowd, then tucked his head back inside and closed the window. His apartment was warm and comforting and the sunlight shined onto the livingroom floor and spread into the kitchen.

Catherine came out of the bedroom, her eyes swollen

and red.

"I spoke to Father Patrick yesterday," she said. "I told him you would see him today."

"I was hoping you had forgotten," he grinned. Then seeing Catherine's eyes, he lost the grin and got up from the couch. "You've been crying," he said. "I hate it when you're sad. I hate seeing you sad everyday."

"I told him you would see him this afternoon," she said. "He'll be at the church until two o'clock. I said we would be there around noon."

"Frank Beatrice wants to talk to me sometime today," he said. "I haven't spoken to him since Wednesday."

"I don't like him," she said. "I know I said it before but I can't like him. He makes me sad too."

"I hope you will not be sad again," Harry said. "I hate it. This will make you happy this afternoon if I go to church?"

"Yes."

"Good then," he said. "I can't wait to go."

Catherine smiled, and it brought some brightness back into her face.

"You will like Father Patrick," she said.

"I will like anyone if it makes you smile," he said, and leaning in, kissed her lightly on the cheek. Catherine smiled again, her eyes still red.

***

They walked over to Waterloo Street and into the *Cathedral of the Immaculate Conception*. Harry thought it was a long and complicated name but said nothing to Catherine, who smiled as they walked. She was excited and she walked with vim and held his hand tight when she led him up the low stone stairs to the church.

Once inside, Harry unbuttoned his jacket and stood at the back for a moment. The church was empty and it was quiet and dark. Harry remembered how he felt as a boy with his mother, and he remembered the same quiet in the air, his mother walking slowly and delicately, trying not to make a sound. He remembered how she held his hand firm so that he would be quiet as well. And now he felt Catherine holding his hand the same way.

Candles burned at the front on the far wall near the first row of pews. They flickered gently and the light glowed up the wall, then faded into the top of the wall and ended where the high ceiling arched inward toward the middle. Harry's eyes soon focused on a large crucifix behind the altar. He looked at it for a short time without blinking, then followed Catherine up the center aisle where he sat in the front. She lit one of the candles and sat down beside him.

"What's that for?" he whispered.

"For you," she replied. "I said a prayer for you."

"That was nice."

Catherine let her hand fall onto Harry's lap and she smiled at him, a sad smile with her lips pressed together.

"It feels safe in here," he said.

He thought of the family from Romania.

"Do you think there's a higher law in a church?"

"Yes, of course," she said. "If you believe in this you must believe there is a higher law."

"It does feel safe in here," he said again. "I don't re-member it feeling this way when I was a boy. My mother made me feel safe, but maybe it was the church."

"It could have been both," Catherine said.

"Even if I didn't believe in any of it?"

"I think so," she said. "This is a safe place for any-one."

"I feel uncomfortable being here and not believing."

"Relax," she said softly.

"I am relaxed," he said. "But I feel odd. Do you think I'm crazy?"

"No."

"Is it a bad thing to feel odd in a church?"

"No," she said. "Not at all. Lots of people feel odd in church."

"Why?"

"I don't know."

Father Patrick came out from a side door under the crucifix. He was young and handsome with a pointed face, his hair parted neatly to the side. He was dressed in black pants and black shirt with the white clerical collar. Catherine stood up and tugged at Harry to stand. Father Patrick put out his hand and Harry shook it.

"Hi," Harry said.

"Hello," Father Patrick smiled. He looked at Catherine and smiled more.

"I'll be outside," she said.

"You aren't staying?" Harry frowned.

"You two talk alone," she said. "I'll come back when you're done."

"It's cold."

"I'll walk over to Brunswick Square," she said. "Maybe buy a book."

She turned and walked away. Harry felt more uncomfortable in the church without Catherine, and the quiet made him nervous in front of Father Patrick, who sat confidently looking at him.

"Is Patrick your first name?" he asked.

"No," Father Patrick said. "My first name is Joseph."

"Like Jesus' father," he grinned.

"Yes."

"You see I am not completely ignorant," he went on. "I used to go to church all the time when I was a boy."

"Catherine has told me," Father Patrick said. "And you never believed in any of it? Not even when you were young?"

Harry did not expect the question so soon and he sat back against the hard pew.

"There's only so much you remember as a kid," he said. "But no, I don't think I ever did. Maybe in the beginning when I was very young, but I don't know for sure."

"Do you mind if I ask you why?" Father Patrick asked, his voice confident but soft in the quiet of the church.

Harry turned and looked at the candles and tried to think which one was his.

"I just didn't," he said. "There's no reason. I still don't. Why do I like the Leafs? I don't know, but I do. It's one of those things that don't have a reason."

"The Leafs," Father Patrick muttered and smiled.

"Do you watch hockey?"

"All the time."

Harry was impressed by this and immediately was more comfortable.

"You a Leafs fan?"

"Boston," Father Patrick said.

"Jesus," Harry started to say, then cut it down to "*Geeze*...not even going to make the playoffs this year."

"They're young," Father Patrick said. "Joe Thornton is going to be good."

"Thornton is good and he's strong," Harry said. "And he's only getting better."

"And they have good young defence," Father Patrick continued. "Big and strong. Byron Dafoe is good."

"He's inconsistent," Harry argued.

"He isn't Curtis Joseph," Father Patrick smiled. "But he's good. He's got a good glove."

"I suppose," Harry said.

"I've never liked another team," Father Patrick continued. "Always the Bruins ever since I was this high—" and he held his hand out to his waist. "And if you asked me why the Bruins? I don't know. It's just one of those things. I understand how you feel."

"I'm not against any of this," Harry said defensively, looking around the church. "It just doesn't feel true to me."

"I understand," Father Patrick said again.

"You believe."

"Yes."

"Does it feel true to you?"

"Very true," Father Patrick answered.

"That's a good thing," he said. "Am I wrong not believing?"

"No," Father Patrick answered. "It's good to be true to yourself."

"On my way here I thought you would try to make me a Catholic," Harry said.

"I won't stop you," Father Patrick grinned.

Harry smiled.

"I'm only here to listen," Father Patrick said. "I'm not going to talk you into anything you don't want to do."

"You're not at all what I expected," Harry said. "You're young. You know hockey."

"This isn't a convent," he smiled. "I'm a person too. There are a lot of things I abstain from, but hockey isn't one of them."

"Can I ask you a personal question?" Harry said.

"Yes."

"Have you ever been with a woman?"

"No."

"Never?"

"I kissed a girl when I was twelve," Father Patrick smiled. "But no, I've never been intimate with a woman."

"Not a girlfriend in high school or anything like that?"

"No."

"Geeze," he said. "I don't know how you do it. I don't know what I would do without Catherine." And he suddenly remembered himself drunk on the roof in the rain, without her. "And I'm not saying it's only about sex. Catherine's my best friend. She knows hockey too."

"She is a good woman," Father Patrick said.

"You're not the first person to tell me that."

"She cares about you a great deal."

"I know," he muttered. "I think she thinks you will talk me out of tomorrow. I think she hopes you will."

"I'm not here to talk you out of anything."

Harry sighed and stretched out his legs.

"She lit a candle for me," Harry said. He sat a moment and said nothing. Then, turning back to the candles: "I'm going to miss her."

"Sometimes I get lonely and wish I had someone," Father Patrick said. "You are lucky you have someone to miss."

Harry felt uncomfortable hearing this from a priest.

"Did Catherine tell you about tomorrow?"

"I knew who you were before yesterday," Father Patrick said.

"And you aren't going to try and stop me?"

"No."

"I don't understand."

"I'm here to listen," he said again.

"Oh," Harry said.

Father Patrick said nothing. He sat calmly until Harry spoke again.

"It makes Catherine awful sad."

"Does it make you sad?" he asked.

Harry didn't answer right away. He crossed him arms.

"The Bruins could have a contender if they keep the team together," he said.

Father Patrick smiled and let Harry continue.

"They're good but young. Joe Thornton is going to be a superstar. Could lead them to the Cup someday."

"If he continues," Father Patrick said.

"He started out slow his first year," Harry said. "But he was only eighteen, and he was on the fourth line. He played more his second year and did well. And this year he is doing good. I think he'll keep getting better. He'll get stronger and he'll learn how to score the way he did in Junior. The Bruins are treating him right, letting him grow at his own pace. That's the right way to handle a first overall pick. Didn't ruin him like the Senators did with Daigle. Poor kid, now he's laughed at."

"They did put a lot of pressure on him," Father Patrick said.

"Too much," Harry added. "Eighteen years old and they tell him to lead the team. Too much too fast. And it ruined him. It's too bad. He could have been great if he was allowed to develop. But Thornton, he's on the right team, and he'll be great if he keeps going."

"Vincent Lecavalier has that kind of pressure," Father Patrick said.

"I don't think he does," Harry argued. "Tampa Bay has nothing to lose. I'm not worried about Lecavalier. He's got the talent to develop on his own. I think he was better than Daigle as a Junior. And I think he'll be a superstar on his own. The way Jagr is right now, in a class of his own, miles above everyone else. But it will take time. Even Jagr needed that."

They sat silent for a moment, and Father Patrick, seeing Harry was not going to continue, took his turn.

"It hurts you to see Catherine sad."

"Very much," he said.

"Does it make you sad?" he asked again.

Harry didn't answer right away. He looked at the candles again.

"When I think of not seeing her anymore, it does," he said. "I love her. She has cried every day this week and I hate seeing her cry. I hate seeing her sad like that all the time."

"Then why do you make her sad?"

"I want this," he said. "I would give her anything. But this, this is inside of me, and I have one chance at it, to live forever."

"There is Heaven," Father Patrick said.

"That's your belief," Harry said. He was comfortable with the priest now and his words came out easily. "It's not mine. You have your Heaven and your church and that's your right. But it's my right not to believe."

"Yes it is," Father Patrick said. "But God has put you here for a reason."

"You're talking through your own belief," Harry said. "There's no God to me."

"But there is," he said.

"You're preaching to me now," Harry said, standing up. "I think I want to leave now. I don't want to say something wrong."

"You can't say anything wrong."

"I will if I stay," he said. "There are things that shouldn't be said in church, whether you believe or not."

"It sounds like a piece of you believes."

"Catherine has said the same thing," he shrugged. "But there isn't. It's a matter of respect."

"There won't be any disrespect."

"I'm talking about my mother," Harry said. "She believed truly, probably just as much as you. And she would roll over in her grave if I said the wrong thing in here, or to you."

"Please stay."

"I don't think I should be here," he said. "I don't feel right. I don't feel comfortable here."

"Please stay," Father Patrick said again, sympathetically. "You just got here."

"I think it would be best if I go," he said. "Yes, I think I should go."

Father Patrick didn't say anything. Harry shook his hand and walked out of the church and found Catherine in Brunswick Square.

***

When Harry woke up Sunday morning, he could already hear the crowds down on the street. He rolled over on his side and looked out the window. He couldn't see the street for the people squeezed in between the buildings and there was a mass of heads and arms and hands, all tight together. Down the street the heads blended together and it looked like a wave of garbage had swept over the street in all colors. Harry could see signs with HARRY and JUMP! He saw police lights flashing on the corners, and police officers doing the best they could to contain the numbers. He saw in different places men holding T-shirts and people with money in their hands. He saw hot-dog stands popping up here and there, smothered by the crowds.

Then he looked across the street and onto the roofs of other buildings where bodies lined the edges, huddled in jackets and scarves and mittens, shivering in the January cold, their breath clouding out from them as they breathed. Every window of every building was filled with faces, some windows open with heads hanging out.

Harry rolled over in bed and smoked a cigarette and wished the day was warmer, wished it was like yesterday.

"You're awake," he said to Catherine as he lay on his back smoking, his arms lying at his sides.

Catherine rolled over in bed, and stretching out long held the curtain back and looked out the window.

"You see it out there?" Harry said.

Catherine's eyes widened.

"You're a star," she said, looking down over the crowds. "You really are. Look at them. There must be five thousand people out there."

Then instantly her excitement ended and all she could think of was Harry.

"I thought Frank would be here by now," he said. "It goes live broadcast at noon."

Catherine could see her breath clouding in the glass as she stared out the window. She pressed her fingers against her lips and quietly wept. Tears ran down her face and she felt them salty and warm on her lips.

"Will you be on the roof with me?"

Catherine pulled herself from the window and wiped her eyes.

"No."

"Why not?"

"It's real," she sniffed. "It's all too real."

"I need you up there with me."

Catherine started to cry again. She tried holding her tears but she couldn't. When she opened her mouth to speak, she sobbed. Harry lay beside her quiet. She cried for a minute before she could speak.

"I can't go up there with you," she said. "I never believed today would come. I saw you so happy all week and I knew it would end. I knew it would. And now it's here and it's all over. We are all over."

"I'll always be here in the city," he said. "Today I make myself a part of it forever."

"But you will be gone forever," she said. "I will never lie with you again like this. This is the Harry I will never see again."

"I need you on that roof with me."

"I told myself I would be strong for you when Sunday came," she said. "But now that it's here I can't. There's a hole inside of me and all my strength has fallen into it and I can't do anything but cry. And it hurts. It hurts the same as when you think of that boy. It hurts so truly horrible. Oh Harry, do you really have to do this?"

"This is what I've dreamed of," he said. "Of being remembered, of not being forgotten."

"There are other ways."

"No."

"You don't have to do this," she said desperately. "You can talk to someone and things will be better. Things will always be the way they were this week. You can be happy again if you want. You don't have to do this."

"I'm happy now, here," he said; then looking out the window again,"These people need me. And I need them. These are the people who make me a star. They will make me live forever."

"By killing you," she muttered. "I can't be there to see that."

Harry leaned in close and cupped Catherine's hands in his. "If there is anything I have ever asked you for," he said, "it is this one thing. Please, Catherine, I can't do this alone. Can you fill in the hole for just a while longer?"

"I don't know if I can," she wept.

"You can," he said. "I know you can. This is the biggest moment of my life and I want you with me."

Catherine said nothing.

"Will you come up to the roof with me?" he asked again. "Please, Catherine?"

Catherine wiped her tears on the blanket, kissed Harry on the lips, then went into the bathroom without answering. Harry sat on the edge of the bed, his hands on his lap.

She was still in the bathroom when Frank Beatrice came. He had been on the roof an hour already, he told Harry.

"Do you see them on the street?" Frank said. "Do you see how many people are here to see you?"

"I see them," Harry said and sat on the couch. "How many do you think there are?"

"Enough," he said. "Didn't I tell you I would make you a star?"

Catherine came out and sat beside Harry, curling herself up and wrapping her arms around him.

"Some people have camped overnight to see you," Frank went on. "I brought a few of them up onto the roof – maybe have you signing autographs for them in the background when I open up."

Harry listened quietly.

"It's straightforward: I go into speech with you in the background signing for fans. Then up onto the ledge from there and into history."

"I sign. Then onto the ledge."

"I'll take you through it," Frank assured him. "When I'm done speaking, I'll get you. You don't have anything to worry about."

"Catherine is coming up onto the roof," Harry said. "I want her there."

"There will be a place for her to stand," Frank said. "How are you doing?"

"I'm fine," he said. "A little nervous, but fine."

"It will all be over before you know it."

"Can I ask you something?" Harry said.

"Sure."

"I read the story about you taking the job in Toronto. Is it true?"

"I have been considering it," Frank answered. "I've been offered different jobs since you have come along."

"But you are leaving Saint John?"

"Possibly."

"You might get to know Harry Neal and Bob Cole," Harry said. "And maybe even Ron MacLean. Will you be doing anything for Hockey Night in Canada?"

"No," Frank said. "I would be working for The National News."

"Oh."

"I don't watch hockey."

"Really?" Harry frowned. "Then why go to Toronto for the CBC?"

Frank rolled his fingers. "Money."

Frank left Harry and Catherine alone and went back up onto the roof. He told Harry he would send someone down after him when the time was ready. Catherine went to the kitchen and made coffee.

"Do you want something to eat?" she asked.

"I'm not hungry."

"Neither am I."

She sat at the kitchen table. The shouts from the crowds came through the apartment.

"Listen to them," she said.

"I hear them."

"They're all there for you."

"I know."

"You're nervous."

"A little."

"You'll be fine," she said. "I'm proud of you, Harry. The whole city is here to see you. I'm proud and sad."

"I don't want you to be sad," he said. "I don't want to make you sad."

"I'm very sad," she said and started to cry again. "I'm trying to be strong for you. I'm trying my best but I'm too sad to think anything else."

Harry went over to her and kissed her cheek. He felt the tears on her cheek, and then he kissed her again. Catherine did not cry when Harry kissed her.

"I'll always be here," he whispered.

"I want you here always," she said. "Like this right now. Here, where I can stand with you and touch you and hold you."

Harry kissed her again and they went into the bedroom.

Harry was cautious with Catherine as they made love, as though she was everything pure and good and he didn't deserve her. But there she was, and he had her, him feeling somehow nervous, like the first time when he didn't know her well and didn't want to make any mistakes. And now everything with her felt new again because it was their last time, not the first, and because he knew he would never have her again.

***

Harry lay beside her in bed. He watched her closely, her eyes closed as she lay on her back. There was a sad smile that bent slightly at the corners of her mouth, a flicker of morning sunlight on her bare breast. He studied her calmly, watching and listening to her breathe in and out, and thinking how perfect she was, there at that moment.

An hour passed and the crowds became louder. Catherine was still asleep when the knock at the door came. Harry got out of bed and left the room. Catherine awoke when he got up, for he had been so still as he lay that it was the first time he had moved since she fell asleep.

Harry came back and sat on the edge of the bed.

It was time.

He dug into the night table drawer and pulled out a handful of money.

"You take this," he said to her. "It's what I've earned this week. Buy a car with it and learn to drive. You're a good driver."

Then he held out his hand and placed his mother's brooch in her lap.

"I also want you to have this," he said. His eyes watered when he spoke and he choked a bit on his words. "I'm not a good man, Catherine, I know that. I never believed in God or the Bible or anything else. This is the only thing I've ever believed in."

Catherine began to cry. She wrapped herself around him.

"Oh, Harry," she wept. "Please don't do this. Please, please don't leave me. Please don't."

"I'm not leaving you," he said. "I'll always be with you. I'll always be a part of you."

"I will always remember you."

"I won't be gone from here," he said. "They'll name a street after me. And maybe even a holiday. I'll always be here."

"I'm trying to believe that," she sniffed, her face pressed into his shoulder as she cried. "I'm trying very hard to believe that."

***

It was cold on the roof and Harry could see his breath. He wished he had worn his jacket but Frank insisted there was no time. Harry didn't understand— it would only take a minute. Yes, Frank had said, only a minute, but a minute could not be spared if everything was to be done right. Harry wanted his jacket. Frank cursed and sent someone down for the goddam coat. Harry didn't like the way Frank had blown up. He saw his breath again and shivered in the cold.

Cheers came from the rooftops when they saw Harry, and from there the street followed in cheers and screams. Cameras flashed and he waved and smiled at them all. They handed him his jacket and he quickly slipped into it. He wanted mittens, he said.

"Use your pockets," Frank said, then he stopped and took a deep breath. "I'm sorry, Harry. You must understand that I'm under a lot of pressure here. I know it's cold. Do you mind using your pockets?"

"No," he said.

"Good," Frank smiled. "Let's work together so everything will be perfect."

"Yes," he said. "I want this to be perfect."

Then Frank turned into Frank Beatrice and took control of the whole roof. There were four cameras, two men with microphones, two men with lighting boards reflecting the sun, and a pretty make-up lady whom Harry had immediately noticed. A dozen or so people who lived in the building grouped together, shivering and sipping on cups of coffee. Two police officers were standing at the roof's entrance, chatting back and forth, looking at the crowds, and seemingly unaffected by the cold.

Frank placed Harry in front of the group of fans who stood shivering, their eyes fixed on him. Catherine gripped Harry's arm tightly. She squeezed him and cried. Frank put his hand on Harry's shoulder. Catherine did not look at him.

"We'll start in a few minutes," he smiled. "Is there anything you want? A coffee?"

"No, thank you."

"Are you alright?" Frank asked. "Is everything alright?"

"Everything is fine," he assured him. "Don't worry about me. Do your thing."

The make-up lady put something on Harry's cheeks and he could smell her perfume when she bent over. Then someone handed him a pair of brightly colored sneakers. *Jesus*, he thought. *All that money for wearing these? Mel could have given me something better.* He laced them up with cold fingers and felt awkward when he stood, as they were light and bounced under his feet.

"Less than a minute," Frank said, his face reddened with make-up, his hair perfectly puffed. "It's showtime."

Catherine did not let go of Harry. She stayed close to him, and spoke into his ear as she cried.

"Don't do this, Harry," she wimpered. "Please don't leave me. Please please please don't. Please no. Let's go downstairs and lie in bed, just me and you. Please don't do this. You can't really do this."

Harry hugged her each time she spoke but he didn't say anything.

He was signing autographs just before Frank started his dialogue. Frank's back was turned to him, and he saw the light from the camera shining the outline of Frank's head as he spoke.

"So you guys camped out to see this?" Harry whispered.

"Since midnight," one teenager said.

"You must have froze."

"It was cold," he said. "But here we are."

"I haven't slept yet," another grinned.

"You must be tired."

"Too cold to be tired."

"Thank you for doing that," he said. "For camping out. If I had known, I would have brought you down some coffee or something. This winter weather is terrible. It would be better in the summer."

"I was there," a young woman said suddenly.

"Where?"

"I was there in the summer when Devon McGrady was killed."

Harry stepped back. "You remember his name?"

"Yes," she said.

"Did you know him?"

"No," she replied. "I was there and I remember seeing you. And now look at you; you're a superstar. I can't believe I'm here talking to you. I can't believe I'm standing here talking to Harry Cossaboom."

Harry dropped the pen. The two teenagers standing beside him fell to their knees and another two fans scuttled down to get it. They wrestled over it until one of them had it.

Harry thought a moment. *Frank said nobody would remember him. Nobody would remember Devon McGrady. He said they will remember me. Will they? Will they forget me?* He thought of Charlotte Street and himself and Catherine there in the middle of the night. He remembered the walk back home, and Charlotte again, *Charlotte.*

No no, don't think of that. It's too late for that. This is your day, Harry Cossaboom. Your day alone. These people are all here for you.

Or are they?

Yes, yes they are. All here for you.

He looked at the crowds gathered on the rooftops across the street. *No, they aren't. They're here for a piece of you. For a pen or an autograph. They're not here for you. They don't even know you. They won't know you from a street sign. They won't know you from anything. They have never known you. They don't even know you're real. Are you real? Yes, yes you are, you foolish prick.* He looked down onto the street. *But why don't you feel real?*

Then Frank Beatrice stopped his thoughts. Harry turned quickly and saw Catherine crying, her hands on her mouth and her eyes red. She pressed her face into Harry's chest and wept, her grip tight around his arm.

"This is it, Harry," Frank said into his ear. "It's time."

Catherine would not let go. Harry turned and hugged her.

She held her head up and looked at him. Her eyes were swollen red, her cheeks rosy in the cold and wet with tears.

"Don't do this," she sobbed. "Don't do this to yourself, Harry. Don't do this to me. I don't think I can live without you."

"You'll be fine," he said.

"No I won't," she said quickly. "I can't live without you. I don't want you to leave me all alone. Don't do this. Please don't leave me."

Harry felt his eyes filling with tears as he pulled himself away from her. Catherine's mouth was wide open. She started to cry so hard she couldn't cry at all. Her face trembled and her lips hung lifeless from her open mouth, like a drowned man pulled from a river.

***

The crowds on the rooftops and down in the street went wild when Harry stood tall on the ledge. He waved around and a stream of flashes went off. He felt a small warmth inside his body and waved again, and again the crowds cheered and more flashes went off. He breathed in the cold air and turned and saw Catherine crying. He looked up to the sky and it was blue, but some clouds had blocked the sun and the air was cooler without it.

Harry had not seen the open patch down on the street. Police officers lined the area, making sure it stayed clear. When he did finally see it, everything around him stopped. He didn't hear the crowds, didn't feel the cold, didn't feel the bounce under his feet. He didn't think of Frank Beatrice or the make-up lady who smelled so good. He didn't think of the cameras rolling behind him, nor the ones on the street pointing up toward him with shining lights. He didn't even see his breath. He felt only one thing— his heart pounding against his chest. He felt the blood pumping fast up through his neck and pulsing against the collar of his jacket.

What have you gotten yourself into? he thought, panic coming into his head.

He looked back at Catherine who had her hands up to her face.

The crowd started chanting Har-ry!—Har-ry!—Har-ry!

Harry felt a thin line of sweat down the middle of his back and took off his jacket and dropped it behind him.

The crowd cheered again.

When Catherine heard the crowd she couldn't take it anymore. She took one last look at Harry on the ledge then dashed toward the door, slamming it against the wall.

Harry turned when he heard the door open. He didn't know it was Catherine who had gone. He turned back around when the crowd brought him back. He thought of the week. *The sky blue in the morning. The sun shining in my room and lighting everything, Catherine there beside me and I touched her and kissed her and held her close beside me. And she would smile at me and she would lie there still and perfect and she was all mine.*

And now all that is gone. All that is gone forever. What have you done?

He looked around to the screaming crowds.

What have you done to these people? What have they done to you? You're a hard old fool, Harry. A hard old fool and there's nothing you can do about it now.

His chest was tight and heavy, his throat swollen when he swallowed. He felt tears coming into his eyes but forced them back. He bit hard on his lip until he felt the warm taste of blood on his gums. His fists were clenched tightly and he felt the palms of his hands moist, the outsides of his fingers cold and stiff. He turned around slowly and looked for Catherine.

She's gone, he thought. *Where did you go?*
You're gone.

I'm sorry. I'm so sorry. I put you through this and now you're gone. You were strong to come up here. I love you, Catherine. You're a strong girl and I love you. You dear sweet thing. I will always love you. And I will always be with you.

Harry turned back to the crowds across the street and far below. Then back around again, looking for Catherine.

She's gone, he thought again. *She's really gone.*

Then, down Orange Street and across the tops of the buildings, Harry saw the opening of King Square. And he saw the tops of the old trees poking through, reaching up slightly above the buildings, the tips swaying back and forth in the wind.

He turned again, hoping to see Catherine.

I don't want to die, he thought suddenly. *I want to see Catherine again. I want to wake up tomorrow morning with her in my bed and see her smile and have her kiss me. Why didn't I listen to you, Catherine? Who was I then? I would do anything to have that again. I'll believe in God. Do you hear me, God? If you can get me out of this I'll believe you. I will. You can add me to your list of believers and I'll be a good man.*

He looked down once again to the bare patch on the street.

That's what I'll do. If there's a God he'll set things right. I'll give the money back to Mel's, to Chizzlers, to Irving. Give it all back. I'll pay them more if they want, more yes, more. Nick would help me, he would. Give me what I need. I could get a job, get anything, then pay Nick back, yes yes yes! And Catherine will be with me forever and ever. I'll do anything, God. Anything to get me out of this. You save souls and mine needs it now. I'll marry Catherine. And we'll marry in a church and you will be there with Jesus too. Yes, Jesus, I believe in you. Can you help me? Please, dear Lord God, please? Can you hear me?

He thought of his mother, and being in church with her when he was a boy. He remembered her leading him to their pew and whispering to him to keep quiet. He remembered her brooch and how she looked like a fairy tale.

Mom, can you hear me? Can you help me, Mom, please? Please, can anyone help me? Is anyone there?

Harry felt hope come into his body for a moment when he thought she was listening. And in this short moment the cold sank back into his lungs and he breathed deeply in and out, fast, then smooth, and the freshness of the cold air inside of him took all that was heavy out. The tightness in his chest broke, the air loose and free and flowing in and out. He breathed wonderfully, felt the blood in his veins, down his legs and into his toes, then up through his arms and down into his fingers tingling. He smiled brightly and his eyes opened fully and his ears felt the cold and heard the wind around him, the wonderful wind and the cold.

I'm here now. Right now. And this is what's what. Catherine, I'm here. I can breathe today, and breathe it with you. I'm me and me alive.

He looked across the rooftops and saw all the many faces lined together, glaring with hopes and cheers. Then he looked up to the sky where the sun had broken through the clouds. He spread his arms out wide and closed his eyes and felt the cold air on his face, the sunlight on his cheeks. He felt his heart slow against his shirt and in his silence he found a place where life, here and now, was so very good.

***

A hand slapped down hard on Harry's shoulder and he opened his eyes.

It was Frank Beatrice.

He put his arm around Harry and set his chin over Harry's shoulders so that their faces were close together.

"Well," Frank said. "This is it."

"I don't know," Harry said.

"You don't know?"

"No."

"It's a big step to take," he said. "Very big."

"I don't think I can do it."

"Take your time."

"I don't think I want to do it."

"Nobody wants to die," Frank said.

"I wanted to once," Harry said. "But not anymore."

"We talked about this, Harry."

"I don't care about that."

"Do you want to go back downstairs to your apartment? Remember what that was like? Remember what you told me? About waking up every morning and nothing changes? You want to go back to that? You want to go back to the same thing every day?"

"It won't be like that."

Frank paused for a second.

"Are you better now, Harry?"

"Yes," he said. "I want to live. I want to live and be happy."

"Can you be happy?"

"Catherine makes me very happy. She makes me feel alive," he said. "All I need is her."

"Women are wonderful, aren't they?"

"Yes."

"My wife makes me happy," Frank said. "She bitches

and bitches but when it's all said and done, I don't think I could live without her."

"What's her name?"

"Leigh."

"That's a nice name."

"Yes it is," he said.

"Does she make you want to live?" Harry asked.

"If she doesn't kill me first," Frank grinned. "I can get under her skin sometimes. I'm not the easiest guy in the world to live with."

"I like seeing Catherine beside me in bed in the morning," he said calmly. He pictured her in his head and forgot the crowds below. "I used to wake up and wish I didn't. I wished the day would get out and leave me alone. Now when I go to bed I can't wait for morning to come so I can see her there beside me. I watch her when she sleeps and I feel like I'm the luckiest guy in the world. She makes me want to live forever."

"You can live forever now, with all of this," Frank said.

"But I want to live right now," Harry said. "I want to live today. I want to see Catherine today, every day. I want to feel her with me and feel her beside me in bed. I want to wake up every morning with her. I taught her how to drive. She was laughing and smiling and I was there beside her and I was laughing and smiling too. I want to be with her for everything she does, when she smiles and laughs, or even cries. She is the best woman in the world. She is everything good. I want to be right there beside her. That's what's real to me. I don't care about this anymore. This is all wrong. There is nothing real about this, about any of this."

Both stood quiet on the ledge as the crowds grew impatient. Everything got louder with each passing minute.

"We've worked very hard all week for this," Frank said. "I've worked hard."

"I know you have," Harry said. "And I'm sorry to let

you down. Will you still get the job in Toronto?"

"Don't worry about me," he said. "Worry about you. I'll manage just fine."

"You want that job, don't you?"

"More than anything."

"You won't get it unless this all works, will you?"

"Probably not," Frank said.

"I'm sorry, Frank."

"Is this really what you want?" he asked.

"Yes," Harry answered. "Things are very different now."

"But you'll be just the same. And it will go on the same until you get fed up again and sooner or later you'll end up right back here on the ledge. Except nobody will be here, Harry. Nobody. There won't be any cheers; you won't be anything. Just a drunk up on the ledge like you were before."

"It won't be the same," Harry insisted. "I know it won't. Not no more."

"Have you ever been to Toronto, Harry?"

"I've been to Montreal."

"Well I've been to Toronto," Frank said. "And now they want me. They're watching us right now, you know. Everyone is watching. You're a real star now."

"I don't care about that," Harry said again. "Right now the world is here and here I am in it and there's nothing more real than that."

"It's a good thing to be in love," Frank said.

"I don't want to die," Harry said. "Not any more."

"We all die, Harry. But you, you can go out on top of the world."

"I don't care," he said again. "I'm getting down from here. I'm going to find Catherine and marry her and have kids and live my life here and now."

The sun came out from the clouds once again and a wind blew across their faces.

"It's nice up here," Frank said. "I never realized how

much you can see."

"You can see a lot," Harry said.

"I never knew the water ran out that way," Frank said. "I bet you can see the tip of Nova Scotia on a clear day."

"Maybe."

"I bet you can."

"I like it too," Harry said. "To be able to see above everything else."

"It is nice," Frank said again. "It relaxes."

"It does," Harry said. "It would be better in the summer though, when it's warm."

"It would be great in the summer," Frank said; then turning around and looking at the others on the roof, added, "Maybe a barbecue up here, with this view."

They said nothing for a moment.

Frank shivered.

"Jesus it's cold."

"Let's get down from here," Harry said. "I don't like it as much as I used to."

"Alright."

"What about all these people?" he frowned. "What will happen with them?"

"I'll take care of that," Frank said. "Don't you worry."

Harry sighed and relaxed. He didn't mind the crowds now.

"Let's get down," Frank said.

"I thought you would be mad."

Frank smiled slightly. "It's nice to know you're better now."

"Thank you," Harry smiled.

Frank smiled warmly. "Thank you, Harry."

He kept a firm hold around Harry's shoulders, and Harry felt Frank's grip tighten. Then Frank pressed his arm hard against the line of Harry's back and wavered forward.

Harry's eyes widened.

His arms swung out but he could grab nothing.

And Harry fell, the wind blowing strong against him, the rushing wind in his ears high and white as he fell, his clothes flapping violently against his body. No ground beneath him anymore, no ground above him, he fell down and down, slicing the cold as he went, the crowds cheering loud.

***

Catherine did not feel her legs as she flew down and around the staircase floor after floor. When she arrived at the bottom floor, she swung open the door and stepped out onto Orange Street. She was startled when the crowd gave a sudden roar that echoed off her chest and sank itself deep inside her.

Harry had jumped.

Not long after that cold January day, Orange Street became a place of local legend, where Harry Cossaboom stories could be heard in every store and around every corner. And in the summer months, those who lived on Orange Street gathered on their rooftops where they could see the dry dock that had once flourished with shipbuilding but was now desolate and still. And the toll bridge that crossed the river into the West Side of the city. The pulp mill with the long trucks coming and going. And not far from Orange Street, between the old brick buildings, they could see the tops of the old trees in King Square.

Author's photo by Nelson Rosa

Jerrod Edson was born Saint John, New Brunswick in 1974. He is now completing his BA in English Literature at Carleton University in Ottawa. *The Making of Harry Cossaboom* is his first novel.